# A Whole Lot of Bar-B-Q

and other Baseball Stories

# *A Whole Lot of Bar-B-Q*

## and other Baseball Stories

by

# Mike Shannon

# Dedication

For baseball art super stars Scott Hannig and
Donnie Pollard, with admiration and gratitude
for kindnesses I can never repay.

# Also by Mike Shannon

**Hutch: Baseball's Fred Hutchinson and a Legacy of Courage,** Illus. by Scott Hannig (2011)

**The Good, the Bad, and the Ugly Cincinnati Reds: Heart-Pounding, Jaw-Dropping, and Gut-Wrenching Moments from Cincinnati Reds History** (2008)

**Willie Mays: Art in the Outfield** (2007)

**Baseball Books: A Collector's Guide** (2007)

**Coming Back to Baseball: The Cincinnati Astros and the Joys of Over 30 Play** (2005)

**Baseball in Chillicothe: Images of Baseball** (2005)

**More Tales from the Dugout: More of the Greatest True Baseball Stories of All Time** (2004)

**Everything Happens in Chillicothe: A Season in the Frontier League with Max McLeary, the One-Eyed Umpire** (2004)

**Riverfront Stadium: Home of the Big Red Machine** (2003)

**Tales from the Ballpark: More of the Greatest True Baseball Stories Ever Told** (2000)

**Tales from the Dugout: The Greatest True Baseball Stories Ever Told** (1997)

**Willie Stargell: Baseball Legends** (1992)

**The Day Satchel Paige and the Pittsburgh Crawfords Came to Hertford, N.C.: Baseball Stories and Poems** (1992)

**Baseball: The Writers' Game** (1992); expanded edn. (2002)

**Johnny Bench: Baseball Legends** (1990)

**Diamond Classics: Essays on 100 of the Best Baseball Books Ever Published** (1989)

# Contents

# The Baseball Boyhood
# of Spider Cleaver

The only son of Art and Ellen Cleaver had a disturbed childhood growing up in Jacksonville, Florida, that North Florida river city with megalopolistic aspirations forever frustrated by its large redneck population. Jacksonville has always been more of a football than baseball town, but that didn't prevent the Cleaver boy from becoming totally obsessed at an early age with the game of sphere and ash. His first glove, his first backyard home run, and baseball cards, both the kind he bought for a penny apiece (stick of gum included with each card) at the local 7-Eleven and the kind he cut from the backs of Post cereal boxes, got him hooked.

What drove him over the edge was juvenile baseball literature, those 1950s-vintage adolescent biographies of everybody from Joe DiMaggio to Richie Ashburn. The Cleaver boy read them all. And then he *lived* them all. The lives of Sal Maglie, Yogi Berra, Stan Musial, and others became his life; their deeds became his deeds; and their personalities became his personalities.

Understandably, Art and Ellen at times felt they hardly knew their son, but they told themselves it was just a phase he was going through.

Since Jacksonville did not have a major league team of its own to root for, the Cleaver boy was free to grant his allegiance to any team. He adopted the Washington Senators for two reasons: he liked the logo on their baseball cards, a pitcher superimposed on the Capitol, and he admired the men who not only played major league baseball but who also were leaders of their country at the same time. The Cleaver boy was thus the only kid in the country not living in Washington, D. C., who dreamed of playing for the ever-lowly Senators; a team so unpopular that nobody ever guessed what the "W" stood for on the cap the Cleaver boy always wore.

Because of all his reading the Cleaver boy understood that a nickname was de rigueur for anybody serious about getting to play in the major leagues. He gave his neighborhood pals lots of hints, but when it became obvious they were oblivious to their duty, he gave himself the nickname "Spider" because he imagined he spread a web-like coverage over the shortstop position. "Beanpole" would have been more realistic for the tall and lanky lad, but who ever read a biography of a big leaguer with such an unheroic nickname?

One hot day in July when Spider was a mere ten years old, he told his mother he wanted to spend some of his bonus money for turning pro to buy her a great big, brand new house to take her out of the poverty of the ghetto. Ellen thanked her son for his generosity but felt compelled to point out that while she and Mr. Cleaver were mortgaged up to their eyeballs, they weren't exactly living in the poorhouse either.

Another time that summer Spider's next-door neighbor, Nancy Pitts, who'd just begun wearing a training bra, asked him if he wanted to go down to the 7-Eleven for slurpees and said that after that they could go steady if he wanted to. A fresh constellation of freckles on her face made Nancy look cuter than ever, but Spider said no, he was saving himself for a Hollywood actress.

The biggest day in young Spider's life came the next spring when he made the San Souci Saints Little League team. In those days kids actually got cut from Little League teams, and Spider's friend Porky was one of the unfortunate kids to feel the ax that day. After everyone else had left the Saints' practice field, Porky sat on the bench sobbing bitterly. Compassion welled up in Spider's heart. He remembered reading in those adolescent biographies how so many of the big leaguers had begged when they were youngsters, to be allowed to carry the equipment of the professional ball players who had been their heroes from the stadium parking lot to the locker room, and he offered to let Porky carry his glove and bat to the Saints' first game on Tuesday night. Porky stopped sobbing and picked up Spider's Vic Wertz Little League model bat, but at the last second he restrained himself from bashing in Spider's skull. Instead, Porky called Spider "an All-American jerk-off" as he mounted his yellow stingray bicycle and peeled off, spraying pebbles and grains of clay in his wake.

That summer and the next Spider lived for Little League baseball. He wasn't the best player in the league or even the best player on his team or even the best player at his position on his team, but he showed he knew how the game was supposed to be played.

He got thrown out of two games for cursing the umpire and got ejected from another for throwing dirt in the face of an ump who had the nerve to call him out on a close play at the plate. One night a four-eyed s.o.b. on Osterman Optical brushed him back three pitches in a row, and Spider had to head out to the mound, bat upraised, to show the league's pitchers that he couldn't be intimidated.

He also made his last Little League game a memorable one when he tripped and fell down trying to catch an infield popup and his chewing tobacco got stuck in his throat. Spider crawled around on his hands and knees for a few moments, gasping and gagging and turning blue before his coach picked him up and whacked him on the back. Spider then spit out a huge brown glob which the coach's whack had dislodged. Alarmed parents who had rushed onto the diamond were momentarily upset that a Little League participant had even been allowed to chew tobacco, but upon closer inspection the brown glob turned out to be only candy, an ersatz chaw made up of 15 nougats of dark caramel and nuts.

After Spider's Little League career ended, he continued to play as much baseball as he could. He gradually noticed some of the rest of his life, but he never outgrew his baseball dreams. The scouts were there at his high school games wearing banlons and loafers, sitting in a clump behind home plate, balancing notebooks on their knees, but Spider was more impressed with them than they were impressed with him. The plain truth was that he was a mediocre ballplayer in high school and a step-below-mediocre in college. By that time Spider finally realized he would never make the major leagues, at least not in baseball, but he did get to Washington. Georgetown University, to be precise, from which he graduated with a master's degree in political science.

Shortly thereafter, Spider finally entered the real world, gaining a seat on the Jacksonville City Council in his first try. In the type of abysmally hackneyed language that would be used to describe a succession of Cleaver races, a local political pundit writing for the *Florida Times-Union* declared, "The brilliant campaign run by Dwight 'Spider' Cleaver was a clear (and clean) home run and marks this hometown hero as a young phenom worth watching."

In the following seasons Spider moved up through the political ranks like a hot prospect tearing a path through the minor leagues. He never did marry a Hollywood starlet, but he did wed a comely holder of the

Miss Florida crown who could put on a hell of an act when she wanted to, and just as he turned 33 he gained a seat in the United States House of Representatives. The Cleaver family gave Spider a rousing send-off back to Washington, celebrating like they had just won the World Series. Ellen doused him with champagne, and Art kissed him on the forehead. Spider felt like he was going home.

In our nation's capitol Congressman Cleaver rolled up his sleeves and attacked the work before him like a new manager trying to rectify the problems which had been keeping his ballclub mired in the second division. The word quickly spread around town that the new Congressman's style of management was Lasorda-ish. He insisted that his staff call him simply "Skip" or "Skipper," and he often rewarded a job well done with a bear hug, a pat on the rear, or a double "high five." Around the office he wore his old Washington Senators cap, and his memos, directives, and speeches were filled with the rhetoric of America's national pastime.

The Congressman worked long and hard trying to reduce the deficit, improve public education, and bring some relief to the families of the over-burdened middle class. He also tried to remain sensitive to the needs and desires of his constituents back in North Florida and to build the bipartisan grassroots support he would need to one day win a seat in the United States Senate.

But most important of all, he lobbied continually and passionately for baseball to put a team back in

Washington. He attended scores of rubber-chicken dinners a year just to say, "Every batter since the dawn of time, including that most famous of all Casey's, has received his duly-apportioned number of strikes. This great city has missed two pitches but has one big strike left. I remind the baseball powers-that-be of the lesson I learned on the sandlots of Jacksonville, Florida: 'It only takes one pitch to hit.' I've said it before, and I say it again to you tonight, 'Bring the Senators back to Washington.' "

So you see, although it may have been perverted, Spider Cleaver's boyhood was not wasted.

# The Charlie Pepper Letters

*Tallahassee, Nov. 4. 1980*

Dear Mr. Corrado:

You will have to excuse the inexcusable delay in my answering your letter of Aug. 17. Since my retirement I am afraid that I have become lazy and a great procrastinator. After all those years of working under pressure to meet some paper or other's deadline, it is a real pleasure to spend the day puttering around the house doing practically nothing at all or watching some of the teams over at the University. I am a big Seminole fan these days.

Your project on the Reds teams of '39 and '40 sounds exciting; that was a great ball club, and it's about time that somebody has thought to do a book about them.

I will be happy to help you in any way I can, as long as you stick to what happened on the field. In my day we figured what a fella did on his own time after the game was his own business and not something to embarrass him with by making headlines out of—as the practice seems to be today.

I suppose there's very few people still at the *Enquirer* who know me as more than just a name payroll sends a check to every month. It's nice to be remembered though, and I thank you for the kind words about my work in Cincinnati.

Sincerely,

Charlie Pepper

*Tallahassee, Dec. 15, 1980*

Dear Mr. Corrado:

I am glad that your work on the book is going so well. I apologize for the tardiness of this response, but preparations for the holidays—especially Christmas card writing—have kept me very busy.

You are right about the Reds catching: it was the best in the league. All you ever hear about anymore is how great Johnny Bench is. Everybody except old timers like me seems to have forgotten how good Ernie Lombardi was. Bench is a great one, that's for sure, but he never won a batting title like Ernie did. (Actually, Ernie won two: one for the Reds and one for Brooklyn). Ol' Schnozz could really handle the bat, and if he'd had any speed whatsoever he'd have batted a good 25 or 30 points higher every year. The infielders played Lombardi so deep—knowing they had extra time to get the throw over to first base—that it was like batting against 7 outfielders.

The fellas on the team really looked up to Lom too. He was a real leader on that club, not a phony rah-rah type, but somebody all the guys respected and looked to in the clutch. Ernie took a lot of friendly kidding about his nose and his slowness a foot, but there wasn't a more loved man on the team.

Harry Danning of the Giants was a terrific catcher in those days too, and, of course, Gabby Hartnett is in the Hall of Fame though he was nearing the end in '39 and '40, but I'd still give the nod to Lombardi. The Reds back-up catching, as you said, was also "unusually" good.

Well, that's about it. Hope these notes help with the book.

Sincerely,

Charlie Pepper

*Tallahassee, February 8, 1981*

Dear Mr. Corrado:

Your theory about the dissension on the Oakland A's and Yankees teams of the '70s being the catalyst that led to their championships is interesting, but I would guess that they won in spite of all the bickering, not because of it. There's no substitute for talent in the big leagues.

Concerning the '39-'40 Reds, there WAS no dissension that I was aware of—besides the usual (and natural, even inevitable) minor friction that develops whenever a group of 25 men are thrown together and have to live together for a stretch of 8 or 9 months.

Good luck with the book.

Sincerely,

Charlie


*Tallahassee, Feb. 20, 1981*

Dear Mr. Corrado:

In my opinion Bill McKechnie was a great manager, absolutely deserving of his niche in Cooperstown. Winning pennants with three different organizations (a major league record, by the way) is hardly a matter of "being in the right place at the right time." He had baseball smarts, and he knew how to handle a ball club. He got the most out of all his ballplayers, and they played as hard as Ty Cobb trying to win for him. The fellas on that club loved Bill McKechnie, and he treated them like sons. You don't see that kind of bond much in professional sports anymore.

As you probably know, Mr. McKechnie was a very religious man (sometimes called "Deacon Bill"). He was a patient, kind, understanding man whose word was nevertheless always law.

I'm not sure I know what you seem to be hinting at in asking whether I think he made "any serious errors"; over a 154 (or 162) game season every manager makes some moves that backfire, but I don't think anybody could have done a better job with that team than Bill McKechnie.

Sincerely,
Charlie


*Tallahassee, February 27, 1981*

Dear Mr. Corrado:

No, I don't mind if you call. However, please don't phone in the evening as my wife and I retire rather early.

Charlie


*Tallahassee, March 4, 1981*

Dear Mr. Corrado:

As I told you on the phone yesterday, I am not eager to discuss Willard Hershberger. His suicide is still a disturbing memory, and as I told you from the beginning I think a ballplayer's personal life is off limits for a writer—even after he (the ballplayer) has passed on. Let me add that in my day I believe we had more respect for people and their dignity than writers do today. We certainly never viewed a tragedy or another man's misfortunes or mistakes as an opportunity to advance our own careers, and I think we handled Hershberger's death properly; that is, as delicately as possible.

I would not like to see Willard's suicide sensationalized even now—after so many years have passed by. However, if you give me your word that you will treat the matter respectfully and if you let me see your manuscript before you send it off to the publishers, I will discuss it with you — to a point.

Sincerely,

Charlie


*Tallahassee, March 10, 1981*

Dear Mr. Corrado:

Yes, you have the basic facts concerning the "Hershberger case," as you put it, correct. One reason I've always been reluctant to discuss the matter is that people can never seem to keep the facts straight. Something always gets distorted or fabricated. Even several days after Willard had killed himself and we had already put down the basic circumstances in the *Enquirer* as simply and as accurately as we could, there were wild rumors going around.

One rumor had it that Willard had killed himself over a New York show girl who had spurned him, and another had it that a beautiful female fan had murdered him because he jilted her. Both rumors, as you know, were equally ridiculous. I guess they both had something to do with Hershy's (his nickname, by the way) reputation as a ladies' man. Years later I heard a man old enough to know better say that Willard "blew his brains out because he had dropped a third strike that cost the Reds the Series." When people don't even take the trouble to get a story like that straight, they don't have much business going around gabbing about it.

There's really not much I can add to what you've learned by reading the old *Enquirers*. We put down what we thought propriety and decency allowed and what was sufficient to inform the public, and we left it at that. Although finding the body in the bathroom gave me a tremendous shock and made an impression on me that I have never been able to forget, I see no reason to bring up in your book the graphic details of the deed.

Sincerely,

Charlie


*Tallahassee, March 20, 1981*

Dear Mr. Corrado:

You've raised a very interesting question which is also a quite sensitive one. And it is a question I am certain everyone who had daily contact with Hershberger then has asked a million times since.

I suppose the reason no one saw it coming was that the suicide was such an exaggerated response to what Willard was feeling or experiencing that there was no way for anyone to conceive of such a thing really happening. The fellows knew Willard was depressed about the game he supposedly lost for the team in New York—he felt like he had called the wrong pitch—but nobody blamed him for Danning's home run. Hell, Danning was an All-Star player, and though he was a cousin of Bucky's, no pitcher gets his patsies out ALL the time. Nobody even dreamed of putting any blame on Hershy for that—not even Bucky who took the loss (in the ninth, after leading 4-1, I think) very hard. (I will never forget Walters just standing out on the mound, staring up into the stands with a blank look on his face, all alone while the NY fans are going crazy.)

And then you have to remember that the team was in a race at the time. The boys had almost been caught the year before in '39 by the Cardinals, and they were definitely feeling the pressure in August of 1940. To make things worse, Lombardi was out with an injury (that's why Willard was getting so much playing time), and the heat that summer was unbelievable—I don't remember a hotter summer in my life. All these things kept everybody's mind occupied and a bit on edge, and I guess Willard's depression just looked like what everybody else was going through, maybe just a little worse.

Besides all this, Willard was basically a loner. He was friendly and usually pretty cheerful, and he was popular with the team and the fans, especially with the ladies, but he was not very gregarious.

After it happened, everybody, of course, felt just terrible, even sick about it. But nobody could be blamed for anything. There was just no way to see it coming.

I hope these comments help you with this footnote in the story of the '39-'40 Reds. Please remember your promise to give me a chance to approve the Hershberger segment of your manuscript before you submit it.

Sincerely,

Charlie


*Tallahassee, April 21, 1981*

Dear Mr. Corrado:

Although I don't remember the remark and can't find it in my notes, if you read it in the *Enquirer*, then I will vouch for it as I had editorial control over our coverage of the tragedy and did most of the writing myself anyway.

I realize how Hershberger's saying "My father committed suicide and I will too" must look from this distance, but as I said in my previous letter there was just no way to foresee him taking the action he did. Even if anybody on the club did hear Hershberger make such a statement, they would surely not have taken it seriously—nor should they have been expected to since ballplayers say things every day they don't mean.

Sincerely,

Charlie

### A *Whole Lot of Bar-B-Q* and Other Baseball Stories

*Tallahassee, May 8, 1981*

Dear Mr. Corrado:

Yes, of course, Mr. McKechnie knew that Willard was upset about the loss in New York, and he became very concerned when three of four days later in Boston Willard was still worrying himself about that game. But I don't think even Mr. McKechnie realized how upset the boy really was until the night before it happened.

We lost the opener in the series with the Bees, and then something unusual happened in the second game. Willard was catching, and somebody bunted the ball in an obvious sacrifice situation right out in front of the plate, and Hershberger didn't make a move to field it. Naturally, everybody was stunned, especially Mr. McKechnie who called time and ran out onto the field to ask Hershberger if anything was wrong. Willard said, "You bet there is. We'll talk about it after the game." There wasn't much for Mr. McKechnie to do but leave it at that, so he went back to the dugout. That night they got together over dinner and had a long talk. That is when Willard told Mr. McKechnie he was contemplating suicide. Nobody knows what else was exactly said during their meeting, but they talked well into the night, later in Willard's room at the hotel. The next morning, however, I had breakfast with Willard and he said that Mr. McKechnie had given him "a dandy pep talk" and that he felt much better, that he was no longer depressed.

So there again it was just totally unexpected. I'm sure that Mr. McKechnie was still concerned about Willard, but his spirits did seem to be improved, and as manager Mr. McKechnie had 24 other ballplayers to worry about too—not to mention the Cardinals, the Giants, and the Dodgers.

I have tried so many times since then to remember every detail of that morning to recall whether I was concerned by Willard's words and behavior at breakfast. I must not have been because I don't remember being suspicious that anything was amiss.

Later that day at the park when Mr. McKechnie told me what the situation was, I did become alarmed. As you know, Willard never left the hotel that morning to go to the ballpark. When Gabe Paul, the club's traveling secretary, called him to ask why he wasn't at the park for batting practice, Willard said he was sick. Mr. McKechnie asked him to get dressed and just come to the park to give the boys some moral support. Willard said he would but still hadn't shown up by the time the first game was over, so Mr. McKechnie asked me to go over to the hotel to check on him.

The maid let me into Willard's room. When we found the room empty and the bathroom door closed, I knew then for certain that something terrible had happened. But, curiously, I never suspected even for a second that I would find Willard Hershberger on the other side of that door with his throat cut.

There really is nothing else that I can tell you about Hershberger. Surely you know enough to cover this tragic episode in your book, and I trust that it will receive a relatively minor treatment in the book overall. It is always better to concentrate on the positive, and there are many happy, fortunate things about that ball club for you to accentuate.

I am afraid that this correspondence is beginning to wear me out, and to be truthful I am glad that we have gotten to the end of it. I will not take long in editing the part of your manuscript about Hershberger.

Sincerely,

Charlie

*Tallahassee, May 24, 1981*

Dear Mr. Corrado:

Yes, I am afraid that there is nothing to do but take the motivation for Willard Hershberger's suicide "at face value" as you put it. I am not qualified to psychoanalyze anybody, and I refuse to try. I would even balk at applying the word "abnormal" which is a psychiatric term. Besides, this is the sort of prying into a person's privacy that I've told you before I don't believe in. I will say that as far as I'm concerned Willard Hershberger was as normal a human being as I ever met. He was an excellent backup to Lombardi—even though his arm was a little weak—and he had a great career ahead of him. It was just a tremendous shame that he didn't live to achieve it.

So, again, if there was anything beyond his feelings that he was bringing the ball club down that caused his suicide, it will have to remain a mystery now.

Please send the manuscript so that we can tie things up. My wife and I are leaving town on vacation soon, but I will be sure to return it to you before we go.

Sincerely,

Charlie

*Tallahassee, June 2, 1981*
Dear Mr. Corrado:

This is my final letter to you. I have not been happy with the direction in which your questions have been leading, and I resent the insinuations contained in your last letter. I have been quite honest with you from the beginning—which is more than I think can be said for you in your dealings with me.

No, I see nothing "callous or avaricious" in the team's ability to win the pennant and World Series after the tragedy. Aren't you aware that they voted a full share of their take in the Series to Hershberger's mother? And, I told you before that there were many wild rumors surrounding the death of Hershberger, and that business about my finding and destroying "a suicide note" is one of the most irresponsible that ever got circulated.

I now doubt that you will ever send the manuscript to me to approve of, and so I wash my hands of any responsibility for the contents of your book. I insist that you leave my name out of the book's credits, and I urge you not to slander the good name of Willard Hershberger or anybody else connected with his unfortunate and sad demise by speculating on things that you don't know anything about and which are destined to remain a mystery forever.

Sincerely,

Charlie Pepper

# Cubs Win! Cubs Win!

I was sitting around the office one dreary day this past March, trying to keep my mind on my insurance business. There'd been an ice storm the night before—like winning baseball, a pretty unusual thing for Atlanta prior to the '91 season—and as the morning wore on and the temperature rose, clumps of ice slid off tree branches and telephone wires, exploding on the cars and the pavement in the parking lot.

I was preoccupied with a personal matter, a daydream really, that was symbolized by a little hardback book on my desk called *A Wife's Guide to Baseball* by Charline Gibson and Michael Rich, "with notes from the mound by BOB GIBSON." The dust jacket showed two female hands (Charlene's presumably) choking up on a long white bat.

When my secretary, Sandra Granger, an efficient 32-year-old mother of three (nonsmoker, tennis player, health food nut ... excellent life insurance risk), came in around lunch time to remind me about my afternoon appointments, I realized that I'd spent the whole morning fantasizing about meeting Wendy, about ... as crazy as it sounds ... tracking her down.

After Sandra left for lunch, I decided to do it. I picked up the phone and called Seattle, Washington. It was a long shot, but maybe Carlton could help me.

"Is this Carlton Winegardner, the Daniel Boone of baseball book scouts?" I said. I could picture Carlton rousing himself for business, brushing cigarette ashes off the sleeves of his plaid flannel shirt and clearing a place among all the books, catalogs, and newspapers on his desk for him to open a notebook and take down an order. With his ruddy face, wire rim glasses, and stringy gray beard, chubby old Carlton looks exactly like what he is: a professional book scout and book dealer. The only detail out of character is the Seattle Mariners baseball cap he wears, a dingy blue hat featuring the Mariners' much-too-clever, obsolete logo, a trident inside a star. Unlike Sandra, Carlton, who is 41, is not a good risk. He drinks too much, he smokes like a fiend, and the only exercise he gets is rolling the dice in his weekly Pursue-the-Pennant league games.

"Yeah, this is Carlton. Who's calling please?"

"This is Curt Jaster in Atlanta."

"Oh, great! I was going to call you this afternoon. I've got you a copy of *The Curse on the Cincinnati Reds*. It's almost a perfect copy and it's signed by Dick Wagner and Marge Schott, so I'm going to have to charge you $75. Is that okay?"

"Yeah, sure. I'll take it."

"I could get more for it, and I could sell ten copies of it if I could find them, so it's no problem if you want to pass on it."

"No, no. I'm glad to get it, and I think the price is fair."

"Okay. I'll send it out tomorrow morning when I take a bunch of orders down to UPS. Hey, Curt…"

"Yes, Carlton?"

"How can you spot a level-headed Braves fan?" Carlton loves to tease me with jokes about the Braves. After the jokes I always remind him that I'm a die-hard Cubs fan merely living in baseball exile, but he ignores that little technicality. I guess he figures I'm guilty by association just for living in Atlanta.

"I don't know. How can you spot a level-headed Braves fan?"

"He drools from both sides of his mouth." As usual, Carlton got a huge kick out of his joke, but after he laughed himself out I skipped the comebacks about his Seattle Mariners-induced inferiority complex and told him I needed some information about a book I thought he'd sold me, a little thing called *A Wife's Guide to Baseball* by Charlene Gibson, wife of Hoot.

"Hold on, Curtis. Lemme check the old Apple here, and I'll tell you what you want to know. Here it is. Yep. I sold you that book. Set you back four bucks."

"When?"

"Three years ago."

"Where'd you get it?"

"Now that I'm not sure. The Apple doesn't tell all. But I can look up where I took buying trips that year, and that's probably how I picked it up, if that would be of any use to you to know."

I waited for him to continue.

"Let's see, I went to D. C.—my sister got married there—to Philadelphia—my 20th high school reunion—and to Cincinnati."

"Why'd you go to Cincinnati?"

"Oh, I just thought it might be a fertile area."

"Was it?"

"Not really. Not for baseball books anyway, ha, ha. I remember picking up a couple of boxes of the usual stuff but no finds."

"Carlton, you don't remember anything unusual about the book?'

"No. Is there something special about it that I missed? It couldn't have been signed if I sold it to you $4.00. I mean, by *Mister* Gibson."

"No, it's not signed. By Mr. or Mrs. Gibson."

"Well, what's so special about it, and why are you asking me questions three years later about where I got it?"

"I don't know. Just curious."

"Yeah, well, it's not exactly *The Boys of Summer*, is it? Come on, Curt, now you got me curious. What's an advanced collector like you worrying about a trifle of a book like that? Why do you want to know where I…"

"You'll send *The Curse* out tomorrow, right? Nice talking to you, Carlton."

"Wait a minute, why won't you tell me..."

"Have you started jogging or playing tennis or anything yet, Carlton?"

"I've been thinking about it, Curt, really I have, but I'm so..."

"Well, you better start doing something, buddy."

"Curt, I really want to but..."

"Something's come up, Carlton. I gotta go. Bye now." I hung up while he was still trying to make his excuses. I hated to be so rude—not to mention deceitful—but I was too embarrassed to tell him what was so important about the book.

Wendy Hoerner. Wendy Hoerner. Wen-dy Hoerner. I must have said that name a thousand times in the week between the moment I first saw it in Charline's book and my phone call to Carlton. I kept saying Wendy's name, like a chant or a cheer: "Cubs win! Cubs win!" When I concentrated on the sound of it, I could picture better what Wendy looked like.

I first saw Wendy's name, written in pencil in a meticulous feminine handwriting, when I picked up *A Wife's Guide to Baseball* after knocking it off a bookshelf in the baseball room of my condo in Decatur, Georgia, a suburb of Atlanta. The Cubs' Cactus league game in Mesa was on WGN. Some guy the Cubs had just picked up from the Yankees was starting in right field. I'd never heard of the guy, so I was going to look him up in *Total Baseball*, but when I tried to pull *TB* off the shelf *A Wife's Guide to Baseball* popped out and fell on the floor. I started to put the little book back, but then I noticed the inscription on the flyleaf: "Given to me for my birthday by Roger, September 10, 1974, at Bluff Lodge, Doughton State Park, North Carolina—on the Blue Ridge Parkway, milepost 241.1."

Who, being a virile unmarried male with a passion for baseball and its immense historical recordability, would not have been intrigued and moved by the innocence and devotion explicit in such a documentation? Suddenly, my hands and feet were sweating, my stomach knotted up, and I felt a little faint, like I was a Little Leaguer stepping up to bat for the first time ever. I gave the book a quick fanning with my left thumb, and I could see Wendy's presence throughout the book, little bits and pieces of her on almost every page.

I saw that Wendy hadn't just read the book that Roger had given her. She had consumed it, taken it apart, studied it, questioned it, and marked it up with underlinings, brackets, arrows, stars, exclamations points, question marks, and cross-reference numberings as if she were going to be tested on the material. I had never seen a baseball book taken so seriously before. And to think that such an eager, dedicated student was a woman!

I sat down on my chair embossed with the seal of the Hall of Fame and read from cover to cover both Charline Gibson's book and Wendy Hoerner's running commentary on it.

If you've ever read the book, you know it's a real primer, that "Charley" (as Gibson calls his wife) assumes almost no knowledge of baseball whatsoever on the part of the reader. For a seasoned fan, the majority of Mrs. Gibson's careful explanations of rudimentary aspects, rules, practices, terms, etc. would be totally unnecessary and tiresome, but I was fascinated to follow Wendy's reactions to them.

Wendy obviously learned a lot from the book. In fact, she found it so instructive she read it twice; marking it up the first time in pencil and the second time in yellow highlighter. She wasn't a complete novice when she started though. Even the first time through she wrote comments in the margins that indicated a certain level of familiarity with the game, such as the appreciation she expressed for Charley's description of the way the infield throws the ball around the horn after an out is made: "Beautiful ... such close observation!" There was no way of telling how much time elapsed between her readings, but there were clear indications of her progress. Instances of her ignorance and confusion ("Is this the same as hit-and-run? Ask Roger") decreased, while instances of her knowledge and confidence increased ("Right! But don't forget the set-up men").

When I finished, I laid the book down and looked up at the big screen across the room and saw not the Cubs and Brewers in Kokoham Park, but Opie Taylor and friends playing cowboys and Indians while Andy tried to get some paperwork done at his desk in the Mayberry courthouse/jail. I'd been reading for almost two hours. With a twinge of pleasurable guilt I thought, "That was more like reading a young woman's diary than a baseball book."

While Barney (at Andy's desk) sweet-talked Juanita (at the diner) over the phone, I mulled over the things I did not know. I didn't know where she was now. I didn't know how to find her. I didn't know what I'd say to her if I ever did find her. All I knew for certain was that I was in love with Wendy Hoerner.

The fact that this woman was probably married didn't bother me in the least. I figured I'd deal with that later if it were a problem. I had to find her first, or it made no difference anyway. Besides, there was at least a 50/50 chance she was divorced now. My marriage hadn't lasted, hadn't lasted even five years. I'd been looking for "Miss Right" ever since, so why was it so far-fetched that Wendy might be the ex-Mrs. Hoerner by now and also looking for someone to share her life with? I had a hunch about this thing, that Wendy and I were destined to meet, just like I had a hunch that this was going to be the Cubs year to go all the way.

The information I got from Carlton was hardly a map to Wendy's house, but it was something to go on. That and the name "Hoerner." I first tried contacting all the bookstores in Washington, Philadelphia, and Cincinnati. Nobody remembered selling a copy of *A Wife's*

*Guide to Baseball.* There was no Wendy Hoerner listed in the telephone directories of those cities, nor did any of the few Hoerners listed know of any Hoerner named Wendy.

My ads in *The Sporting News* didn't do squat. I knew going in that *The Sporting News* was a sentimental place to start; real baseball fans don't read it anymore. I got serious when I ran the ad in *Baseball America*, the de facto "bible of baseball" that comes out of Durham, North Carolina. Still nothing though after six straight issues. At the same time I was running ads daily in the *New York Times*, the *Washington Post*, the *Philadelphia Inquirer*, and the *Cincinnati Post*. Just when I was about to switch from *Baseball America* to *Baseball Digest*, the *Cincinnati Post* ad paid off.

The call came one morning around the end of July while I was studying the Cubs' box score in *USA Today*. I was in a good mood because the Cubbies had won five straight to pull within a game of New York and Montreal, tied for first. Sandra buzzed me and said, "Mr. Jaster, I think this is the call you've been waiting for. It's in response to the *Cincinnati Post* ad."

I punched into line two and suppressing my excitement said flatly, "Curt Jaster. Can I help you?"

"Is this the guy that's looking for Wendy Hoerner?" Although it was a bit coarse, the voice was definitely feminine, and my heart raced like a runner going from first to third.

"Yes, is that you, Wendy?"

"Hey, man, hold on a minute. I've got to get some answers to my questions first." I didn't want to converse with the caller without knowing whether she was Wendy or not, but I couldn't risk alienating her and having her hang up. "Okay. Go ahead," I said.

"How do you know Wendy Hoerner?"

"We're old friends," I lied.

"How come you don't already know where she's at?"

"We've just lost touch. I knew her a long time ago."

"How long?"

"Oh, fifteen or twenty years ago, I guess."

"Where did you know her from?"

I knew I could easily blow it on this one, but I'd already decided that the caller wasn't Wendy. I was *praying* the caller wasn't Wendy. I took a stab at it. "I used to live in Cincinnati."

"Oh, so you knew Wendy and Roger?"

"Yeah, sure. My wife and I used to go to Reds games with them," I lied again.

There was a moment of silence. Had I blown it? Was the caller Wendy, and had she sniffed out my ruse?

"Wendy ain't married to Roger no more, you know," the caller said.

"No, I didn't know," I said truthfully. "I'm sorry to hear that," I lied once more.

"Yeah, she got divorced about ten years ago. She's not even living in Cincinnati anymore."

"That's the conclusion I'd come to. Listen, it'd be a lot easier if I could talk to Wendy myself. Why don't you…"

"Yeah? Well, maybe Wendy don't want to talk to you. And don't try to weasel out of the reward. You don't get no more help til I see the five hundred."

"Sure. A deal's a deal. I wouldn't think of reneging."

The caller finally identified herself as Alva Jackson, a friend of Wendy's living in Cincinnati. She said that she'd tell Wendy I was looking for her, as soon as I came across with the reward. That same afternoon I mailed Alva a money order for five hundred dollars to a Cincinnati post office box and waited. Alva wouldn't give me her phone number, and she was not listed in the Cincinnati directory.

Five days later I was still waiting. If the Cubs hadn't won four of five to take over first place in the division, I'd have gone nuts with anticipation. At the end of the week, I had Sandra start calling the Jacksons in the Cincinnati directory, all eleven columns of them. No luck. Nobody knew an Alva Jackson. By the end of the third week, I was so desperate I ran another ad in the *Cincinnati Post*:

Alva Jackson: you have not lived up to your end of the bargain. By accepting payment you have entered into a legally binding contract. Please render the service for which I paid or I will be forced to take legal action against you.

On the day the ad ran I spent the last part of the afternoon over at the McCarvers, writing up a damage estimate. Under Betty McCarver's supervision 16-year-old Nelson had gone around the block a few times with his fresh learner's permit in his wallet. Trouble was, when Nelson neared the end of the driveway, he stepped on the accelerator instead of the brake. Caved in the garage door and did a major job on Betty's Honda too.

Anyway, when I got back to the office, Sandra was gone, but she'd left a note for me on my desk. "Call Operator 6 in Chicago to get in touch with Wendy."

I immediately returned the call. Chicago! What could this mean but that Wendy was living there now? Maybe my luck was about to change big time. Maybe I was about to speak to a woman who loved baseball as much as I did. My ex and I had never had much in common besides a physical attraction to each other. I didn't begrudge Phyllis her interests, but my absorption with baseball and especially with the Cubs gradually got to her. When we got divorced she told the judge that my life, apart from work, revolved around the fortunes of the Chicago Cubs and that when I wasn't watching them on TV, I was reading about them, playing table-top dice baseball games, wasting time at baseball card shows, etc., etc. All that was true, I admit, but I didn't necessarily agree that I had "bored our marriage to death."

"Go ahead, sir," said the operator.

"Wendy Hoerner?" I said cautiously.

"It's Wendy *Washburn*. I dropped the name when I dropped the bum."

"Oh, right, right."

"Say, what's this all about, buster? First, you put some weird ad in the paper, saying you're looking for me because you think I might be a baseball soul mate, whatever that is, and then you get an old girl friend of mine I haven't even talked to for at least five years all hot and bothered that you're going to sue her and…"

"I had no intention of actually suing Alva, but she didn't contact you like she was supposed to. You see…"

"Yes, she did. She called me right after she got your money. I just didn't bother to call *you*. It sounded too freaking weird. And I only called you this time to tell you to get off Alva's back. I don't know how you know me, but I'm really not interested in…"

"Wait a minute. Please hear me out. I know this all sounds a bit weird, as you say, but all I want to do is take you to a baseball game. I know you're a baseball fan, a *hardcore* fan, and I bet you're a Cubs fan too."

"So, what's the big deal? Everybody in Chicago is a Cubs fan."

"I knew it," I fairly shouted. "I'm a huge, huge Cubs fan, the biggest, in fact. I never miss the Cubs when they come to Atlanta." I waited a moment. She didn't say anything. Maybe I was winning her over. "Look, I'd just like to go to a game in Wrigley with another real Cubs fan, that's all."

"Well, Mr. Jaster, I know I don't know you, but what's bugging me is how do you know me? We've never met as far as I can remember. How do I know you're not some pervert or psycho that maybe has taken secret photos of me on the street and has them plastered all over your room at the YMCA?"

"Wendy, we have met before, sort of, but it would be hard to explain how to you over the phone. I'm not a pervert or psycho, believe me. I'm an honest, hard-working regular guy, and not all that bad-looking either. I own my own insurance agency here in Atlanta. I'm single now but I was married once. To tell you the truth, I don't blame you for being a little suspicious."

"A 'little' suspicious? I'm a *lot* suspicious."

"Okay. I can understand that. All I'm saying is that I'd like to meet you and that I can explain everything better in person, especially at a baseball game. The Cubs have a long home stand coming up in the middle of September. Let me take you to a game then. Say, Saturday the thirteenth against the Cardinals. Maybe, if they stay hot, we can see the Cubs clinch the division that day," I joked.

I paused to catch my breath. I could tell she was thinking it over. "Come on. There'll be 40,000 people at the game. What can happen? If you don't like me, if you don't have a good time, we'll go our separate ways, and I'll never bother you again. If you do have a good time, maybe we can go out to dinner after the game. My treat, of course."

"You're going to fly up to Chicago just to take a perfect stranger to a ballgame?"

"Yeah. Why not? Stranger things have happened ... like 1969."

"Maybe so, but not to me."

I was disappointed she didn't catch my clever allusion to the Cubs' famous choke in '69 when they blew the divisional title to the Mets, but I pressed on.

"So what do you say, Wendy?"

"Okay. I'll go to the game with you. But I'm warning you: I'll have mace in my pocketbook."

"Sure, sure. You can use it on the Cardinals." I laughed, but she didn't.

Of course, there was no chance of Wendy and me seeing the Cubs clinch on the thirteenth. Still, with our hootin' and hollerin', we would be able to help them extend their lead over the tenacious Mets to four full games with sixteen to play.

Wendy and I were to meet on the corner of Clark and Addison, across from the famous sign that proclaims : "Wrigley Field. Home of the Chicago Cubs." Naturally, the game was a sellout, but I had been more than happy to pay $100 for a pair of great seats. In a second call right before I flew up, I'd given Wendy a description so that she'd be able to pick me out of the crowd. She wouldn't give me a description of herself. I guess she figured that if she didn't like the way I looked she'd just walk right on past me and stand me up.

At six-foot-six, 190 pounds I'm pretty hard to miss … unless you look at me sideways. The Cubs cap I was wearing to hide my baldness on top didn't set me apart from the crowd any, but nobody else that I saw was wearing a genuine flannel Cubs jersey. The day was a real scorcher, and I was burning up in the flannel and the blue baseball sleeves I had on underneath, but I thought it would be worth it. The flannel I was wearing once belonged to Ted Abernathy, and people tell me that I kind of resemble the old submariner with the big ears and longish face. I try to take it as a compliment. I thought the flannel jersey would make me a dead giveaway, but Wendy never showed until the starting lineups were being announced. I caught sight of her as she approached me from the right.

She was about six feet tall with flowing reddish-orange hair and was wearing a flowery sack dress that accentuated some rather large hips and breasts. She wasn't carrying any pocketbook, so I guessed I didn't have to worry about being maced. She was older than I'd imagined—she might have been 45—but her freckles and sparkling green eyes invigorated her countenance.

"What's the matter? You were expecting Madonna, maybe?" she asked with an unmistakable sneer.

I realized that a look of disappointment had crossed my face. Don't be stupid I told myself. You've had blonde, petite, and beautiful before, and it didn't work out. Besides, this isn't about physical attraction anyway.

I reached out to shake her hand and blurted, "No, no. Don't be silly. I just thought you *weren't* you, that you were going to ask me if I had tickets to sell."

"Yeah, right," she sneered again but less nastily than before. She had an expression of amused boredom, as if she thought she knew exactly what I was going to say and do before I said and did it.

I took her by the elbow and started walking us briskly down Addison. "I have to admit that I am disappointed by one thing," I said.

"What's that?" she asked with slight interest.

"You're not wearing any Cubs clothing or jewelry!"

"I didn't know that was a requirement."

"It's not a requirement. It's just, well, it's what everybody does."

"I'm not 'everybody.'"

Indeed, you're not, I thought. In a gesture of gallantry, or so I thought, I took off my Cubs cap and placed it on Wendy's head. "There. Now you look official," I said.

Wendy whipped off the cap and inspected the inside as if checking it for kooties. As she was putting it back on she looked up at me, shielded her eyes with her arm, and made a big commotion about my baldness. "God, the glare is terrible. I can't see a thing with the sun flashing off your head. Here, you need this thing more than me." I snatched the cap and put it back on.

As we hurried around the corner of the block, she said, "Where in the hell are we going? The entrances are back there."

"Surprise ... we've got bleacher tickets."

"Oh, that's all you could get, huh?"

"What do you mean, 'is that all I could get?' I paid $100 for these babies. Wouldn't you *rather* sit in the bleachers?"

"It's all the same to me. I just thought you'd want to sit up close to the action in the box seats."

I was a little taken aback by that. "You mean you usually sit in the box seats?"

"I did at the game I went to."

"*The* game? You've been to one game? How long have you been in Chicago?"

"About nine years now. I came here from Cincinnati to move in with my old college roommate after I divorced that cheatin' Proctor and Gamble son of a bitch I was married to."

One game at Wrigley Field in nine years of living in Chicago. Heck, I'd seen more than a dozen games in Wrigley myself the last few years. I was too stunned to say a thing.

The bleachers were packed, but we squeezed onto the end of a row about halfway up the section underneath the scoreboard. As we walked up the aisle, a pretty blonde coed, wearing a purple Northwestern University tee shirt and a Cubs visor, brushed past us. She gave me a dazzling smile and said, "Nice flannel!" "Thanks," I said. It took every ounce of self-control I had not to turn around and watch where she was going.

The game was a pitcher's nightmare, a fan's delight. With the wind blowing out hard, fly balls from both teams were sailing into the bleachers as if we were watching BP, and the lead see-sawed back and forth. In the early innings it became painfully obvious to me that Wendy knew as much about the Cubs as I knew about the Yugoslavian national hockey team. She'd heard of Ryne Sandberg but had no idea what position he played. She also kept calling him "Ryan." Worse, she had no appreciation of the ambience, the camaraderie, or the traditions of the bleachers. Even after I explained why the "bleacher creatures" threw the Cardinals' home run balls back onto the field, she thought it was stupid to give them up. The only thing she did appreciate was the view ... of the center fielders' rear ends. Every time I looked around for the beer vendor, I searched the crowd behind us for the coed in the purple tee shirt, but I never spotted her.

The heat, the beer, the closeness, and the rowdiness of the crowd seemed to loosen Wendy up, and she talked freely about her life in a sarcastic, self-deprecating way. She said she met her husband, Roger Hoerner, in college at the University of North Carolina, dropped out to marry him when he graduated, and followed him to Cincinnati when he got a job with Proctor and Gamble as the brand manager of some dish detergent. When she caught him cheating on her with his secretary, she said she realized what a fool she'd been all her life. She divorced Roger and decided that she'd start living her life for herself, even demanding that Roger take custody of the three kids. She came to Chicago because her old college roommate got her a job with a paper supply company. She never said a word about baseball. When I asked her what her interests were she mentioned dancing, traveling, dining out at exotic restaurants, and reading. What sort of books did she read? Self-help, romances, cook books.

My story wasn't much more interesting. Wendy said that the insurance business sounded as boring as the paper business. When she wanted to know how I knew her and why I was so determined to drag her to a baseball game, I felt too sheepish to say. I told her I'd explain it all later.

By the end of the sixth, with the Cubs ahead 9-7, we'd had five beers apiece. Wendy was soaked with perspiration, and the way her eyelids kept drooping I could tell she was getting either drunk or sleepy or both. "God, the game is taking a long time," she said. I decided to ask her pointblank about the book and what happened to the devoted, passionate baseball fan who'd once owned it. But first I had to visit the men's room.

It was so crowded in the bathroom it took me twenty minutes to get back. I had trouble finding our seats. There was no Wendy where I was certain I had left her. I walked up and down the aisle a few times and finally noticed her sitting three rows back and across the aisle. She was sitting next to a burly, bare-chested, fiftyish-looking man and actually had her arms locked around his big right arm. When Wendy saw me, standing there stupefied, she said, "Oh, look, there's Curt!" She wiggled over to her right, pulling her companion with her to make room for me on the end. I sat down and Wendy introduced us. "Lou, this is Curt. Curt, this is Lou. Lou's a sales executive at Monarch Paper where I work."

"Pleased to meetcha," Lou said without taking the cigar out of his mouth. He shook hands without taking his eyes off the field. The Cubs were batting in the bottom of the seventh.

"Great game, ain't it, Curt?" Lou said. Without waiting for a reply he said, "Okay, that's it for that bum. Bring on the next one. See, Wendy, he's got to change pitchers now 'cause that's his second trip to the mound this inning. It's automatic."

"Gosh, how do you know so much about baseball?" asked Wendy.

"It's nothing, babe. I grew up in this ballpark. Say, where you wanna go for dinner after the game?"

"I don't care. Surprise me." Wendy said.

As Lou delineated his favorite unacknowledged four-star restaurants, I stood up and said, "I'm going to the concession stand. Can I get anybody anything: a hot dog, a pretzel ... an ounce of common decency."

"Nothing for me, thanks. You want anything, Wendy?" Lou said. Wendy shook her head and snuggled up closer to Lou, the paper salesman and baseball expert.

As I walked down the aisle, I heard Wendy giggling as Lou shouted, "Hey, Sandberg, this guy's *meat*. He's *meat*, Ryan!"

What a waste of time and energy, not to mention money, I thought. What a loser you are. You're just like the team you root for! They blew it in '69, they choked in '84, they got humiliated in '89. You should have seen it coming!

I started to leave the ballpark but caught myself. Wait a minute, I thought, you're still at Wrigley Field, and the Cubs, your beloved Cubs, are still winning this game, hammering one more nail into the coffin of the hated Mets, and you're leaving? I walked back up the ramp and out into the mid-afternoon sunlight and worked my way over to the right-center field bleachers. I leaned up against the fence at the back of the last row, just in time to see a Cardinals batter send a rocket into the gap in front of me. It wound up a triple and scored two runs. That made it 11-9, Cubs. A strikeout and a popup brought us within one out of victory. After the Cards' catcher walked on four pitches, Zimmer brought in his bullpen ace. A pinch-hitter, a Latin called up from AAA Louisville, hit the first pitch onto Waveland Avenue, and it was 12-11, St. Louis.

I wasn't worried. The Cubs still had last bat. They had the top of the order coming up and 40,000 loyal, believing fans going crazy behind them. We went even crazier when the first three Cubbies reached on a walk, a misplayed sacrifice, and an infield hit. Then before we'd finished doing proper obeisance to his royal highness Andre Dawson, who already had a pair of homers in the game, the Hawk slapped a grounder down to third. The third baseman fielded the ball and threw it home for one out. The catcher fired down to first to nab Dawson for the second out. Then the first baseman fired across the diamond to third. Shawon Dunston, running from first, had rounded the bag too far! The third baseman took the throw from first, put his knee down to stop the diving Dunston cold, two feet from the base, and tagged him out. Triple play. Game over.

I don't remember a thing about the trip back to the hotel. For all I knew the cabbie circled the block a dozen times to run up the fare. I watched the Mets on cable that night, and they won, cutting the Cubs' lead to two. My flight didn't leave until Sunday night, so I went back to the bleachers for the finale of the St. Louis series. The crowd still had pennant fever and went wild when the Cubs took an early 3-0 lead, but I wasn't fooled. Or surprised when the Cards stiffened, rallied in the middle innings to go ahead 5-3, and won going away 9-4.

Back in Atlanta I watched the rest of the home stand on WGN. The Cubs lost all four to Philadelphia to fall behind New York and oncoming St. Louis. On the road the Cubs started winning again. They played good ball the rest of the season and made it close but finished in third, a game behind New York and two behind the Cardinals, who took the flag. I knew it would work out that way, but I kept hoping, against my better judgment, until the Cubs were mathematically eliminated. It was a depressing way to end the season.

A week or so after the Cardinals beat the White Sox in the World Series I was still fairly depressed when I got a note from Wendy on stationery bearing the Cubs logo. It said:

*Dear Curt:*

*Please forgive me for abandoning you at Wrigley Field. It was the beer and the heat and, I must admit, Lou's charms. Lou really lives and dies with the Cubs, just like you do, and I've never met anyone who knows so much about the sport as he does. I can hardly believe it, but we're getting married next spring. Lou is trying to arrange a wedding at Wrigley Field. However, I didn't write to tell you that. I wrote to thank you for getting me interested in baseball again. I was a big fan a long time ago, but I'd grown apart from the game and forgotten how much I love it. Thanks to you (and Lou, of course) I love it more than ever.*

It was signed "See you in the bleachers, Wendy."

I couldn't get any work done the rest of the day. I felt a whole lot better, but I was antsy as hell. Every half hour I'd pull an old Cubs media guide out of my desk and browse through it until I could force myself to get back to business again. Finally, around three o'clock I gave up and called Sandra into my office. I was taking the rest of the day off, but I told her that before I left I wanted her to book me a reservation for the next Cubs fantasy camp. I was going to put on a real Cubs uniform along with a bunch of other over-30, out-of-shape Cubs fans and get instructions for a week from former Cub greats like Randy Hundley, Fergie Jenkins, Ron Santo, and Ernie Banks. It would cost me $2,500 to go, but I figured that if any Cubs fan deserved to be a happy camper, I did.

# The Day Satchel Paige and the Pittsburgh Crawfords Came to Hertford, N. C.

When the four sleek black Lincolns pulled up in front of the Imperial Hotel, which was Hertford, North Carolina's, only hotel, and a third or fourth class inn at that, a buzz of excitement spread down both sides of the street and snaked through all the doors and windows, immediately drawing outside all the people within. The shiny black sedans were parked directly beneath a canvas banner, stretched over the narrow main street of the town, which enjoined: SEE OUR BOYS WHUP SATCHEL PAGE AND CO. FRIDAY 1:00 MAY 6 AT THE BALLPARK.

Although the 15 occupants of the autos were quite ordinarily black in skin color as expected, the country folk of the small town were very astonished at what they saw as the black barnstormers emerged from their vehicles—which, being the top of the line, were also a cause of amazement. Never had the people of this tiny farming community seen Negroes—or white men for that matter—attired so splendiferously. The black ballplayers, cramped and tightened up from the ride, stretched and flexed, twisted and craned, jiggled and rotated themselves in beautiful handmade suits of various shades of blue, grey, and brown. A few even wore pinstriped suits. All had soft fashionable hats on their heads or in their hands, and their glossy shoes of the finest leathers brilliantly reflected the bright North Carolina sun. Most impressive of all were the sparkling diamond rings that each man wore on his left hand. One older man in the group, moreover, displayed rings of precious jewels on every finger! These were obviously not ordinary Negroes, as one could easily see, by comparing them to any of the tenant-farming Negroes of Hertford scattered up and down the street.

While taking in the spectacle, the townspeople, eager to get a closer look, had all moved towards the barnstormers. They were now bunched around the strangers' autos, from which they kept a respectful distance. Many could be heard asking their neighbor which of the Negroes was the famous Satchel Paige. For the reputation of Satchel's great pitching prowess and of his colorful antics had reached even this obscure hamlet, and it was evident that here, like everywhere else the Crawfords visited, Satchel was the main attraction.

The ballplayers had begun to walk up the steps leading to the entrance of the Imperial Hotel following the portly sweet-smelling man with all the rings on his fingers, joking among themselves about the stir their arrival had caused.

Their progress was halted, however, by a fat white man who took up a blockading stance in the doorway, folding his thick hairy arms across his chest and spreading his pillar-like legs. He was dressed in dingy tan slacks and a short-sleeved white shirt soiled in the armpits and around the collar. On his belt at the waist hung a ring of keys. A supercilious smile broke out across his face as he asked, "What can I do for you boys?"

The black visitors came to an instant halt, each maintaining the place on the steps he had when the fat man had spoken. Some froze with one foot on one step, and the other foot on the step below.

The leader of the barnstorming baseball team, the one with all the rings, said, "I am Gus Greenlee, the owner and manager of the Pittsburgh Crawfords baseball team, members of the Negro League of Professional Baseball. These men are my players."

"Yeah, I know who you are," the white man said indifferently, maintaining his pose and waiting for a further explanation from the black man.

"We have an engagement here to play your local talent in a nine inning exhibition game of baseball at 1:00," continued Mr. Greenlee.

"So?" the white man inquired rudely.

"We played a doubleheader last night in Valdosta, Georgia, and have been driving 11 straight hours to come to your town for an athletic contest. After our engagement here today we are expected in Richmond, Virginia, this evening to play again."

When Mr. Greenlee added nothing further, the white man said with an even wider grin, "Well, that makes you boys the most traveling bunch of niggers I ever seen, but you still ain't said what it is I can do for you."

Mr. Greenlee sighed slightly and replied, "We are thirsty and hungry ... As I said before, we do not need overnight accommodations as we are leaving immediately after our exhibition here. We want only to eat in your restaurant. We have money and will be happy to pay whatever you charge."

Able now to deliver the refusal he had worked Greenlee towards, the white man said with a sneer, "I don't serve niggers in my restaurant."

Several of the Crawfords, resigned to the outcome of this not unfamiliar scene, began to slowly back down the steps. Others bristled at the remark and held their ground.

Without really expecting to change the man's mind, Mr. Greenlee tried again. "We do have money to pay."

"Your money ain't no good here."

"Having been invited to stop here in your town on our tour, is it too much to expect to receive a little common courte—"

"Well, boy, now that's where you went and made your mistake right there. You oughta not go expecting nothing at all, except a good whupping on the ball field. Just because we don't mind showing you who can and who can't play no ball, that don't mean we're changing none of the rules around here."

This pronouncement elicited a few grunts of approval from some in the crowd, but a few others seemed embarrassed by it.

"Ah, Fisk, why don't you let 'em in to eat somethin'," shouted a man in the crowd of townspeople.

"Yeah, after tasting your food, they won't want to eat it no more noways," seconded another.

"I don't let our niggers in here, and I ain't making no exception for these Pittsburgh niggers," replied Fisk adamantly, trying to glare down Mr. Greenlee and his men.

The crowd laughed and began to disperse with the knowledge that the issue was settled, Fisk Harris being the stubborn mule-headed man that he was. These fancy Negroes would have to get something to eat and to drink in the homes of the local Negroes as usual, and, as a matter of fact, just such arrangements were then being made between the Crawfords and several hospitable local blacks. One enterprising old black farmer wearing faded blue denin overalls and a white cotton work shirt was already well into his sales pitch: "... and you can have all the fresh vegetables you want. Corn, tomatoes, sweet potatoes, lima beans, and collard greens. Plenty of honey too for your energy. As much as you can eat and for only fifty cents a man too. You can't beat that so you fellas just follow old Luther out to his place, and I'll see that you get to the ballpark on time too. Mr. Greenlee, you have any objections to these hungry men following me?"

Mr. Greenlee said that he did not, and so about half the Crawfords piled into autos and prepared to drive out to Luther's. While two of the Crawfords were entertaining offers to feed the rest of the team several other players were working out their resentment at the ill treatment accorded them by the white innkeeper who had by now disappeared into the Imperial.

"It ain't right for a man to be able to treat us that way, Mr. Greenlee," said Alvin Cook, the Crawfords equipment manager and bat boy.

"I know it ain't, Alvin. I wish I could guarantee we'd always receive fair treatment everywhere we go, but I can't. You would think though that in the towns where we play, the people would be more gracious, we being like the guests of the whole town."

The players nodded their heads in agreement.

"Why don't we just not play when we're not good enough to be treated like white people? Just move on to the next stop and leave 'em with no competition to play?" asked the angry Cook.

"Well, for one thing, that would mean we wouldn't make no money for this stop," answered Satchel Paige, the wiry veteran pitcher. "And it's their money we'll be taking back to Pittsburgh," he said with a sweep of his long outstretched arm to indicate the people of the small town.

"Yes, and besides that, we've got the reputation of the whole Negro Leagues to uphold. We go skipping out of a scheduled game and that could make it so's that the good white folks wouldn't trust us or no other Negro teams to play the exhibitions as scheduled. And, as Satchel says, that could cost us all some right good money," said Greenlee.

"Just makes me more determined to prove who's better on the field," injected the slender Cool Papa Bell, the Crawfords center fielder renowned for his great speed. "And by the looks of this town, we ain't going to have much problem giving their boys a real good beating."

"No more problem than a whore has sinning," said Satchel. "But look here, we thrash these rubes too bad, we might encounter a little difficulty in making our departure as scheduled."

"You mean like the trouble we had in Kentucky that time you and Leroy struck out all twenty-seven hitters on that coal miners all-star team?" asked Cook.

"'sactly," nodded Satchel. "Leroy Matlock and me humiliated them boys in front of their friends and families. We shouldn't have done that. Black men playing against whites got to be like good doctors—you got to hurt 'em but not pain 'em so bad that they be afraid to come back to see you again."

"That's right. You got to remember that our money might not be no good to some of them, but all their money be good to us," said Greenlee. "Why that fat man will be out to the game today, and his money will satisfy me as much as the next man's."

"Still," said the young Crawfords batbay, his anger defused by the practical arguments of the older men, "there ought to be some way for us to get even."

"Well, maybe there is," said Satchel with a sly wink. "I got me an idea I think you fellas are gonna like."

The Crawfords looked around at each other, exchanging knowing smiles about the resourcefulness and unpredictability of their star player. Before anyone could inquire about his idea, Satchel had already climbed into the front seat of the leading of the remaining two Lincolns and said leaning out the window, "I'll tell you all about it whiles we're eating our lunch."

Hertford's ballpark was not the worst the Crawfords had ever seen, but it was close to being the worst. The infield was a monument to neglect and the ravages of the sun. What blades of grass could be discerned were the color of burnt brown, and on the surface the roots formed what looked like a network of tiny bleached bones. In the outfield and in all the foul territory there was not even the pretense of grass. Worst of all, the infield clay had been baked solid so that hard-hit grounders and sliding would severely test the courage of fielders and base runners, respectively. The seating consisted of two sections of ramshackle wooden bleachers behind first and home for whites and a spare and neglected third section behind third base for blacks. Yet the townspeople of Hertford, having never seen a ballpark any better than their own, had nothing to compare theirs to, and so they were content with it.

By 12:30 practically the whole town had turned out for the game. In fact, so many folks had come to see how Satchel Paige would do against the hometown team (and vice versa) that the bleacher section behind third base had to be used to accommodate the unusual number of white people. And even then the late arrivals had to stand or sit in the sand along the foul lines with the black spectators.

The Hertford team who called themselves the Aces played a crude brand of semipro town ball in a league composed of the Aces and several neighboring towns. The Aces were a perennial contender for first place honors in their league, and it was this tradition that no doubt partly, but only partly, explained the confidence in many of Hertford's citizens that the Aces would spank the Crawfords and the famous Satchel Paige.

Some of this communal confidence melted a bit when the Crawfords strode smartly onto the diamond. If possible, the Crawfords made an even greater impression in their baseball uniforms than they had earlier in the finery of their civilian clothes. The Crawfords' uniform was light grey with red and black piping around the sleeves and the collar, and down the front of the button-down jersey and the sides of the pants. A large brilliant red P in ornamental block style was sewn onto the left chest of each jersey. Black caps and black stirrups with four red rings, along with red baseball sleeves, immaculate sanitary hose, and perfectly shined spikes completed the uniform and created an aura of professionalism and pride. In their motley combinations of farm work clothing, street dress, and odd pieces of baseball apparel, the Hertford Aces, warming up along the first base sidelines, made an embarrassing contrast to the snappy Crawfords. They interrupted their own activities to gaze with a mixture of dazzled envy and nervousness at the Crawfords, loosening up with light calisthenics in front of the third base dugout.

With the Crawfords on the field the undertone of speculation about which of the black players was the famous Satchel Paige swelled almost into a frenzy of anticipation. There were no scorecards for the fans to consult, and as the Crawfords boasted a team full of athletic-looking players there was considerable disagreement in the stands about which of the players in the beautiful grey flannel suits was Satchel Paige. It wasn't long, however, before one astute townsperson pointed out that they would know which player was Satchel as soon as he walked down to the bullpen mound on the left field line to warm up his pitching arm. After this shrewd deduction passed like malicious gossip through the stands, the crowd held its breath waiting for the Crawfords catcher and the great Paige to stroll down to the bullpen mound.

But 10 minutes passed, then 15, and then 20, and still none of the Crawfords made any move towards the bullpen area. The Crawfords continued to throw easily in pairs, play pepper in groups of three or four, and then run short sprints across the infield. The spectators were sincerely perplexed and were beginning to get edgy in their confusion. Why wasn't Satchel—whichever one he was— warming up with his catcher? Was he just going to walk out to the mound practically stone cold and try to get the hometown boys out? These Crawfords seemed to not even have a catcher ... at least none of them was catching with a proper catcher's mitt. Although that husky nigger with the huge arms would make a good target to pitch to.

With only 10 minutes left before game time, the crowd was further surprised by the black strangers when all the Crawfords suddenly left the field and disappeared into the dugout. A silence fell upon the mystified crowd, as the Crawfords were apparently just going to sit in the dugout and wait out the remaining 10 minutes while the Aces, on their side of the diamond, went haltingly through the final stages of their preparation.

It started on the first base side, moved quickly to the center, and by the time it swept to the third base stands, the chant of "SAT-CHEL, SAT-CHEL" was approaching a mad roar. For several minutes no one in the

Crawfords dugout moved. The black ballplayers seemed to be deaf to the chant demanding that their star performer appear. Then, the big husky Crawford, named Josh Gibson, climbed out of the dugout and headed slowly in the direction of the pitching mound on the left field foul line, carrying ... a catcher's mitt! A great cheer went up from the crowd, and the chant of "SAT-CHEL, SAT-CHEL" increased in volume.

When Gibson had walked all the way to the bullpen mound area and had squatted down to assume a catcher's posture, another figure emerged from the Crawfords' dugout. The crowd let out an even greater cheer than before, but it died in mid-utterance as the full figure of a short plump man came into view and headed with a glove on his hand towards the waiting Josh Gibson.

A silence fell over the entire ballpark so complete that one could almost hear the rubbing together of the baggy flannel pants legs of the man in the Crawfords uniform as he waddled down towards the bullpen mound. The Aces were as stunned as the crowd by the sight, and they stood helplessly paralyzed as they watched the chubby middle-aged man with diamonds on every finger toss slow balls from the practice rubber that barely reached the squatting Gibson.

After a few such tosses, the crowd began to come alive again, but this time their tone was hostile and suspicious. Amid the universal booing that began there tumbled down onto the field a cascade of jeers, catcalls, threats, and sarcastic remarks.

"Hey … what are these niggers trying to pull?"

"If that's the great Satchel Paige, my mule can speak French and dance the tango."

"If that Paige nigger don't pitch, I'm a-getting my money back."

"Hell, my little girl Cora would wallop that old black fart."

It was more obvious than ever that despite the miraculousness of there even being an all-black team in the first place that dressed so finely and traveled all over the country playing ball, the imaginations of these country folk had been agitated by the legend of Satchel Paige and would not be satisfied with anything less than the legend himself.

The Pittsburgh Crawford doing the tossing to Josh Gibson—one couldn't rightly call him a "pitcher"— lobbed in his final warmup, and he and Gibson began to head back towards the dugout.

As Gibson and his paunchy teammate neared the Crawfords' dugout, a fat white man stood up in the third base bleachers and bellowed, "That ain't Satchel Paige for damn sure. That old nigger is Gus Greenlee. He's the manager of them niggers I throwed outta my restaurant." Gus merely flashed a big grin, waved a friendly bejeweled hand at the crowd, and flopped down on the dugout bench.

The crowd was now completely exasperated. Their patience had just about run out, and in several parts of the stands—not to mention in the dugout of the Aces—there were murmurs about marching right into the Crawford dugout and demanding some kind of explanation.

The only thing that prevented such action was the start of the game itself. The townspeople had a great deal of curiosity about how the Crawfords hitters would fare against the Aces' ace, a tall string bean of a kid with a bad complexion and a mediocre fastball that was considered by the locals to be a superior one.

The kid's average velocity, in fact, enabled him to breeze through the first. The Crawfords, fine-tuned to hit professional pitching, were way out in front of the ball and produced only two popups and a weak groundout to second. The Aces were ecstatic at this show of competency on their part, and they hustled off the field cheering excitedly for their pitcher and for themselves. The crowd also cheered lustily, and then as the Crawfords took the field, one ... two ... three ... four ... five ... six ... seven ... eight, every member of the town in the ballpark trained his eyes on the Crawfords dugout to see who was left sitting on the bench and to see who would walk out to the mound to pitch. With the eight regular Crawfords at their positions on the diamond, there were five Crawfords left in the dugout, including Mr. Greenlee. Many in the crowd half-expected to see him waddle out to the mound and were surprised—although they wouldn't admit it later—

when a tall, slender, almost awkward Crawford started out of the dugout and shuffled slowly towards the pitching mound.

The tension in the stands was now almost unbearable, and it seemed as if days passed before the black pitcher reached the center of the diamond. When he finally did, he climbed up onto the tall mound, planted his huge feet on the rubber, and faced home plate and the crowd. There he stood not moving a muscle for a full thirty seconds, letting the crowd absorb every detail of his appearance. Then, when each and every person in the stands was about to burst from curiosity and anxiety, Josh Gibson, standing behind home plate, turned to face the crowd. He extended his gloved hand towards the mound and to the suddenly hushed crowd announced, "Ladies and Gentlemen ... presenting ... the ... greatest baseball pitcher of all time ... the one ... and the only ... Leroy ... Satchel Paige!"

Now there issued forth from the throng a mixed cry of relief, excitement, and joy so thunderous that ears of corn were shaken from their stalks a mile away. On the mound in the midst of the sea of noise the black pitcher removed his black cap from his bushy head and made a dramatic low bow to the crowd. Slowly it dawned on the crowd that they had already witnessed a great performance, that they themselves had been the butt of a prodigious gag, one that could have been pulled off only by the inimitable, ingenious Satchel Paige. The crowd began to chuckle sheepishly at its own gullibility; the chuckling soon spread, and in no time at all it blossomed into an outright explosion of laughter. Neighbor pounded neighbor on the back as the fit of laughter continued. Tears of mirth began to form, and sides began to ache from the violent laughing.

The Crawfords too were laughing good-naturedly, and one by one they trotted over to the mound to shake Satchel's hand, congratulating him on the magnificence of his wit. Upon seeing this, the crowd was not to be outdone. They began to applaud the great showman, who had certainly in their eyes lived up to the greatness of his reputation. They resumed their earlier chant of "SAT-CHEL, SAT-CHEL" and kept it up vigorously while the black pitcher threw his warmup pitches.

The Crawfords pitcher now had the townspeople completely under his control. If he had told them to lie down on their backs and cluck like chickens, they would have done so without protest, assuming that it was to be a further part of Satchel's entertainment. When he was ready to begin, Paige held up his hands to command silence, and the crowd responded immediately. When the last mumblings of the crowd had subsided, leaving a perfectly audible silence, Paige began to address the stands:

*Good people of Hertford—you white folks included— allow me to introduce myself. The name is Leroy Satchel or*

*"Satchelfoot" or "Satchemo" Paige from Mobile, Alabama. Maybe some of you has heard of me. If you ain't, you has now and you shoulda before now because I been to more places and won more baseball games than there is of you sitting there. As a matter of fact, I done been to places you never even heard of. They never heard of you there either, but they know who I am. Why, I even been in the company of kings and queens who wanted to make my acquaintance. Now how many of you can say that about yourself?*

*So you see, I may be a black man, but that ain't stopped me from becoming something you ain't—that is, the best there ever was at what I do, and what I do is pitch this here baseball. You ain't never gonna see nobody with the knowledge like I got about how to go about pitching this here ball. Why, I was making fools out of people with this ball before most of you was born, and I'll be making fools out of people when most of you is laying under a cornfield, dead as a worm in a black bird's belly.*

*Seeing me pitch is the eighth through the 100th wonders of the world. That's because I can make this ball do things you won't believe till you see 'em with your own eyes. Seeing me pitch is something you young folks can tell your grandchildren about. You was there when the Pittsburgh Crawfords and Satchel Paige come to Hertford, North Carolina, to play an exhibition game of baseball. Standing here and seeing your faces about to watch me go to work pitching this ball game, I can honestly say that you are the luckiest people in the world and this is the luckiest day of your life.*

Indeed, the people of Hertford must have felt that way because they cheered long and loudly until Satchel again raised his long arms commanding an end to the noise. He then motioned the leadoff Aces hitter into the batter's box and prepared to go to work.

The rest of the game was anticlimactic. Satchel didn't have his best stuff, or maybe not warming up before the game as customary did have an effect on his pitching. Whatever the cause, the lanky black pitcher was not pitching very extraordinarily and gave up enough walks and Texas Leaguers to allow the Aces three first inning runs. Satchel suffered through a shaky second–bases "drunk" and no outs– but the Aces couldn't score, and he found his stuff in the third and began to pitch effectively.

After five innings the score remained 3-0, and it began to look to the hometown fans as if the Aces' kid hurler might be able to shut out the black barnstormers. In the sixth inning though the Crawfords adjusted to the kid's speed and hammered him before he knew what hit him for 11 runs. Cool Papa Bell, Josh Gibson, and the Crawfords veteran third baseman, Judy Johnson, all hit home runs. Bell's was a patented inside-the-park job, and Gibson crushed such a thunderous blast that it not only flew well past the outfield fence in center, but it also crashed through the roof of Horace Jackson's chicken coop another 200 feet away from home plate, upsetting Horace's hens so badly that they couldn't lay for two weeks.

Satchel seemed to get stronger as the game went on. He began to pitch with more and more confidence, trying out experimental pitches, talking to the hitters, disputing their ability, even challenging them to hit the next pitch after first telling them what and where it would be. Although the crowd was totally captivated by Satchel, they still hoped to see their Aces beat the Crawfords; but after the Crawfords scored their 11 runs, their spirits had dropped considerably. In the eighth inning to reinvigorate the sagging Hertford fans, Satchel pulled off another stunt that only he could have dared. With the bottom of the Aces' order coming to bat, Satchel ordered all his fielders off the field. To the howling delight of the Aces fans he faced the Aces with only his catcher to assist him. He then proceeded to strike out the next three batters: one, two, three!

The final score was Crawfords 16 – Aces 3. Although their team had been convincingly beaten, the people of Herford left the ballpark more happy than disappointed because Satchel had put on such a show, living up to, and even exceeding their expectations. To a man they agreed that there was no question about it: those Crawfords, and especially that Satchel Paige, were some kind of special niggers.

Before most of the townspeople could get home or back to their offices or fields, the Crawfords were on the highway traveling towards Richmond, Virginia. In each of the three Lincolns in the Crawfords' caravan hilarity and celebration reigned. In the lead sedan Mr. Greenlee who was driving turned to his passenger in the front seat and said, "Alvin, you could have fooled Satchel hisself today. That was the greatest performance a batboy of the Pittsburgh Crawfords has ever turned in. For a moment there I myself thought that Satchel and Leroy had not gone on to Richmond and that you were really him out there. You really gave those 'lucky people' back there something to remember the rest of their lives, ha, ha."

Alvin didn't say a word in reply but merely sat there grinning, basking contentedly in the praise of his boss and the delirious laughter that flowed over him from the rear seat where Judy Johnson and Cool Papa Bell rolled helplessly from side to side.

# Dead Roses

My first instinct was to start this account with the Little League team I played for in Pensacola and all the Pensacola Wahoo Games I dragged my Mom or Dad to, but nobody wants to hear about those days which are pretty much the same in the lives of all fans who grow up being as crazy about baseball as I am. Notice that I said "account" not "story" because I don't want anybody thinking even for a second that this is made-up fiction, not one word of it. Anyway, I played three years for the Beach Boulevard Winn-Dixie Reds; in case you don't know, the Blue Wahoos in the Southern League were a Reds farm team back then; and in Cincinnati the real Reds had players like Joey Votto, Brandon Phillips, Jay Bruce, Johnny Cueto, and Aroldis Chapman. So it's no wonder at all that, even growing up on the Florida panhandle, I became as big a Reds fan as anybody could possibly be.

I was extremely lucky too. You pretty much have to be to land the job I did. Right out of Florida State University I was hired by Louisville Slugger to be the assistant of the Director of the Louisville Slugger Museum, and the lady I worked for, Jewell Southerland, was exactly what her name suggested. Not only was Jewell pretty and sweet as molasses, she knew what she was doing, and I learned more the first two weeks working with her than I did in four and a half years at FSU. Three years later I got an even bigger break, when the Director of the Reds Hall of Fame retired. Jewell was tight with the Reds, and there's no doubt in my mind that her recommendation is what carried the day for me. She could have had the job herself if she'd wanted it, but she is a Louisville native with deep roots and a patrician family home with big white columns in front and a husband with a good job in town and kids in school there. She wasn't going anywhere, but me, all I had in Louisville besides a great job was a lousy apartment.

Amazing, but true: at the age of twenty-five I found myself in charge of the best team Hall of Fame in the major leagues. The Museum only had three other full-time employees, all older than me. Jim Kates was the Coordinator of Memberships, a sales and fund-raising position; Marty Schmidt was Manager of Programming and Guest Services; and Jessica Lambert was our Community & Schools Outreach person. Jessica's job was similar to Jim's in that her main responsibility was to get people through the doors, in her case school children and other "captive" groups. On a day to day basis I worked the closest with Marty, who was only 30 while Jim and Jessica were both in their early forties, so it's no surprise that Marty and I became pretty close.

As the Director I was supposed to be the big picture guy, the idea guy, but I was in no way a dictator, benevolent or otherwise. I still had to run all significant changes and ideas for new exhibits past ownership and other higher ups. Sometimes my ideas got shot down, and sometimes I had to accept something I wasn't crazy about. Case in point: "Hometown Hubris," an exhibit about the Pete Rose gambling scandal that went up during my second year at the helm. That was definitely an idea I didn't like, an exhibit I didn't want mounted on my watch. I just didn't see the point of dredging back up all that unsavory stuff, and, besides, I'm always in favor of accentuating the positive, not the negative. But as I said, it wasn't just up to me, and there were influential people on the Reds Board of Directors who, for whatever reasons, thought that rehashing the whole scandal would be educational. These were the same kind of people who decades ago convinced the City that a museum dedicated to the enslavement of blacks in America would be a good idea. They named the thing the Freedom Center but everybody calls it the "slavery museum," as they always have, and it's been a bust from the day they opened it. And race relations in Cincinnati? I think it's clear that the slavery museum hasn't done anything to improve them.

The people behind the scandal exhibit also had something besides education on their minds. Fact is, they thought it would be big box office, and they were fine with airing the team's dirty laundry as long as it provided a big boost to the Museum's bottom line. The one thing they never seemed to worry much about during our discussions was the impact the thing would have on the public's image and memory of Rose. I kept reminding them that Pete is one of the most important and beloved players in team history, but they seemed to think that a nice payday would be a sufficient return for a little renewed blemishing of the Rose in the team's bouquet of flowers.

I never saw Pete Rose play—I was too young for that. But my daddy, John Parsons, Sr., saw him play one time in Atlanta. Pete went up to bat five times and got on base all five times, on three hits and two walks. And, yep, both times he drew a base on balls he ran out of the batter's box like a scalded dog on the way to first base. That kind of hustle is what made my dad a big Pete Rose fan, and then my dad made me a big Pete Rose fan by constantly reminding me "That's how you play the game, Son." Major League Baseball may never have forgiven Pete, but Reds fans did, and they forgave him a long time before he died.

Installing a new exhibit is always a lot of work, even when we borrow one already put together. It's ten times worse when we create the thing ourselves. Then we have to do everything. We have to research the topic and diagram the spatial presentation. We have to find the artifacts and memorabilia and arrange to buy or borrow them and then insure them. There's all kinds of contracts and legal agreements to fill out and file. We have to carefully write up a narrative and compose captions to go with all the individual pieces in the exhibit. And the whole time we're doing all this, we have to promote the new exhibit and make room for it by taking down an old exhibit.

Of course, if you're excited about the exhibit you're putting up, it doesn't seem like work. Since I hated the whole idea of "Hometown Hubris," installing it was pure drudgery for me. I called the thing the "Dead Rose" exhibit because we would never have mounted the thing while Pete was still alive. Marty knew how I felt about it, and bless his heart, he worked twice as hard as usual to lessen the time I had to spend on it.

The show went up in a fairly large room on the third floor, on the left, not far from the larger space, farther down, that houses the Reds Hall of Fame plaques. Marty and I spent many a night working overtime, after hours, trying to get the exhibit ready for its opening, scheduled for August first. One night in late July when the Reds were out of town, I was in my office on the second floor working on a caption write-up for the Dowd Report. About three-quarters of the exhibit's artifacts were already installed in the display cases mounted on the walls, and I wanted to refresh my memory as to what page we had our copy of the Dowd Report in the display case opened to. Marty was on the Internet, gathering some basic info on the Federal prison in Marion, Illinois, where Pete did his time—we had some of the prison clothing that Pete had worn—and he barely grunted when I told him I'd be back in a few minutes.

As I walked up the stair case on the south side of the building, I got goose bumps, as usual, looking to my right through the huge wall of windows out at the Rose Garden, a sea of red rose bushes covering the spot where Pete's record-breaking 4,192nd hit landed on the turf of Riverfront Stadium in front of Padres' left fielder Carmelo Martinez on September 11, 1985. The wall of windows on the south end of the building was a stroke of genius on the part of the architects, not only for the Rose Garden view from the staircase but also for the view that those outside of the building get of the 4,256 baseballs, one for each Rose major league hit, that are stacked against the staircase wall behind a three-story sheet of thick plexiglass.

I was so engrossed in thought about John Dowd and Bart Giamatti as I reached the third floor that I looked right at the boy for a moment before I realized that's what I was seeing.

I came to a screeching halt but didn't utter a word, and thinking about it later I realized that was because I was mildly shocked ... that someone was still in the building after we'd been closed for over an hour ... and also because I thought I recognized the kid but couldn't quite put my finger on who he was. I must have stood there, probably with my mouth agape, for half a minute watching him, as he stood in the doorway to the room that would house the "Hometown Hubris" exhibit. He too seemed to be lost in thought as he stared straight ahead into the room, but suddenly he turned his head, looked towards me, and then silently walked into the room. Just as quickly I finally woke up and shouted, "Hey, kid!" as I hurried forward. With my mind racing through possible things I would say to the boy when I apprehended him, I burst through the doorway and into … an empty room. There was no other way out of the room other than the entrance I'd just come through. Nevertheless, there was no boy in the room.

I know it makes no sense, but I moved slowly around the entire room, hugging the display cases and peering into them for some evidence that they had been tampered with or somehow opened, as if the boy might have made his exit through them. At the same time I alternately shot glances back towards the entrance of the room, to prevent the boy, whom I know I had just seen walk into the room, from slipping past me and possibly getting out that way. When I got back to the entrance, I took a look behind me to make sure there was nobody in the room. I looked to the right and then to the left. Nobody. I knew I wasn't crazy, so that meant that somehow the kid had left the room or maybe not even entered it at all without me noticing him—I tried to remember: had I looked away or looked down for a moment while I had walked towards the room? Just to be sure, I walked through the Hall of Fame Gallery where the plaques hang and down the back stairs which lead out of the Hall of

Fame and into the Reds Gift Shop. The kid was nowhere to be found, and the doors that connect the Museum to the Gift Shop cannot be opened, even from inside the Museum, without a key once we close up for the night.

I suddenly realized that the kid might have gone the other way, back through the Museum towards the other staircase and the second floor, so I hustled back there, calling Marty's name once I cleared the stairwell. Marty met me in the office doorway with an alarmed look on his face, which somehow calmed me down. When I told him what had happened, he immediately grasped the situation and, understanding that the kid was trapped somewhere in the building as a key was also needed to open the front doors, he realized we needed to methodically check every nook and cranny on the second and first floors.

Twenty minutes later we were back in the office, seated at our desks, staring silently at each other.

"I'm not crazy, Marty," I said.

"I know you're not, John," he said.

"I saw a kid on the third floor."

"I believe you."

"Then what happened to him … where did he go?"

Marty merely arched his eyebrows and shrugged his shoulders in reply. We sat there a few minutes more, and then I called the cops. Less than five minutes later two of Cincinnati's finest, both black guys, walked up to the front door of the museum. Believe it or not, they had the same last name: Johnson. "No jokes, please," said the thin, light-skinned one, Jerry.

"We've heard 'em all," said his huskier, dark-toned partner, Cornell.

The cops, Johnson & Johnson, made the rounds of the entire museum, just as we had. I answered their perfunctory queries as Marty and I followed behind them. Prompted by their questioning, I articulated, for the first time all night, a description of the kid. I told them he was about twelve years old and was wearing jeans and a white tee shirt. He had freckles and a crew cut, which I'd noticed even though he had on a raggedy red ball cap. And, I was shocked to suddenly remember, the kid had been holding a baseball bat over his right shoulder with his glove slipped over the barrel. The officers halted after taking a few steps up the stairs between the second and third floors. Officer Jerry Johnson bent down and picked up something, a clue perhaps. Marty and I hadn't noticed anything on the steps before, but now we could see, just as the cops did, that the stairs all the way up to the third floor were littered with what Officer Johnson had picked up: red rose petals. And then it hit me. I knew who the kid reminded me of. A snot-nosed, West side, river rat, Keds-wearing Pete Rose.

After the cops left, thinking God knows what about my sanity, I flipped through one of the Rose biographies in the office until I found the photo I was looking for. It was a black and white of Pete in his old Sedamsville neighborhood from 1953.

"There," I said, handing the book to Marty, "the kid looked exactly like that."

"Spooky," said Marty.

It had gotten pretty late by then and we were both too tired and too wired at the same time to do any more work, so we called it a night; but not before I picked up every rose petal on the stairs and shut them up in a small square piece of Tupperware Marty had brought from home.

I stayed home from work the next day, just to relax and get my head back on straight. In the afternoon I visited the Cincinnati Art Museum in Mount Adams for the first time and really enjoyed their exhibit of paintings by the Highwaymen; so called because they were minimally-trained itinerant artists who went door to door selling their garishly-colored Floridian landscapes. I was eating supper and watching TV when Marty called me about half an hour after he closed the place for the day.

"John, could you come over to the Museum?" he said.

"Sure, if you need me to. What's up, Marty?" I asked.

"The rose petals … they're back."

Marty had been on his way up to the "Dead Rose" exhibit on the third floor to put something into one of the display cases that had just come in that day—an autographed ball that Rose had inscribed "I bet on baseball." The rose petals on the stairs stopped him cold. He wanted to check out the third floor but not by himself, and he was happy to follow me up the stairs. When we walked out of the stairwell, I have to admit that I half expected to see the kid again standing right where he'd been the night before. But Marty and I were the only living souls in the building.

After Marty got the disgusting baseball into one of the display cases without our seeing the young visitor from the night before, we felt a little sheepish and started making fun of ourselves to deflate our embarrassment. On the way downstairs we stopped to pick up the new rose petals, and with Marty jabbering away a few steps below me I looked out at the Rose Garden below us and saw the kid, standing there with bat and glove over his shoulder again looking upwards at us. Turning my head to find Marty, I called to him in a shrieking whisper: "Marty, there he is!" When I turned back to the glass wall, the kid was gone. Marty wanted to go outside and look for the kid, but I said no, that we'd find nobody or nothing in the Garden except all those rose bushes.

At this point I was more opposed than ever to the exhibit we were getting close to finishing ... not that my opposition mattered. There was no way the Board was going to change direction this far down the road, so I didn't even seriously consider asking them to. There was no proof that I'd seen anything out of the ordinary, and there might be a logical explanation for the rose petals, although neither Marty nor I could think of one. I also wasn't keen on risking my dream job by making people think I had a screw loose, so I swore Marty to secrecy and hoped that things would just quietly return to normal. Which they pretty much did. Until the day of the opening.

One way a Museum can recoup its investment in an exhibit that they create themselves is to rent the exhibit to other museums. The Board had me doing that with "Hometown Hubris," and I had just finished talking about the show to the Curator up in Cooperstown, Brad Davis. The folks at the National Baseball Hall of Fame & Museum seemed to be interested; unlike, Jewell Southerland in Louisville, who, I'm happy to report, turned the idea down flat. Anyway, Jessica Lambert stuck her head in the office and told me that a visitor, a local school teacher who'd brought her charges to see the new exhibit, wanted to speak to me. Before I could ask Jessica what it was about, the woman stepped around from behind Jessica and directed her complaint right to me.

"You shouldn't have let all the roses out there die like that. It's gross mismanagement or incompetence or something. You know, people do like to see those roses but not like they are now … all brown and shriveled and … dead."

"Dead?" I managed to say.

My emotions must have been plastered on my face because when I looked at Jessica, she simply nodded her head gently and gave me a tender smile of the utmost sympathy.

"Yeah, dead!" repeated the lovely school marm, a short paunchy woman with a generous belly spilling over tight tan slacks. "You need help with the concept? Dead as that squirrel I ran over in my driveway this morning. Dead as my chances of getting the vice principal job at Oyler Middle School. Dead as..."

Before she could supply any more examples to embellish her point, I was brushing past the complainant to go see for myself. Although she could have been nicer about it... a lot nicer ... I could see from the second floor stairwell that the Oyler Middle School shrew was right. We didn't have a single living flower anymore in the Cincinnati Reds Hall of Fame and Museum's famous Rose Garden.

Overnight it seemed this disaster had befallen us. That's what made it so strange, the suddenness of it. As living things, plants and flowers are always subject to a variety of threatening forces, such as weather, insects, disease, neglect; but just the day before our roses seemed to be in the peak of health. What had happened to wipe them out so quickly and so completely?

Charlie Grassley, the Reds' Head Groundskeeper, was as shocked as we were at the devastation. He was also stumped as to the cause, so we turned to the world-famous Cincinnati Parks Department for help. They sent over their best flower man, who also happened to be the Assistant Director of the entire department, a short, bearded Frenchman named Gerard DuMonville. Gerard examined every bush in the Garden and spent three days, practically around the clock, subjecting the dead bushes and the soil to every test known to man. Gerard couldn't pin down the cause any better than Charlie, but he refused to admit defeat, which did not exactly endear him to Charlie.

"Zsahn, zee roses were dee-fective from zee beginning," he told me. "Iz zee only esplanation." I had a different explanation but not one I was willing to share with anybody other than Marty Schmidt.

"Horse shit," said Charlie, as he spat some tobacco juice into a paper cup. "Those bushes been here since the damn ballpark opened. An' we never had no problem with 'em before. What? You think they all committed suicide?"

Gerard said he was not giving up, that he wanted to keep studying the problem, so I had to tell him that the decision had already been made to dig up all the dead bushes and replace them. Even though I thanked him as sincerely as I could for his help, Gerard left my office looking defeated and as disappointed as if he'd dropped a routine fly ball to cost me a perfect game.

Charlie stormed out right behind him, saying, "I ain't got time for this shit. I got work to do."

It took Charlie and some of his crew two days to re-plant the Garden, and when they finished just before sundown on the second day, the Rose Garden was as beautiful as ever. The next morning every single bush was as dead as if some idiot had abandoned them in the middle of the Sahara. It hadn't been cheap to re-plant the Garden, and with the budget as tight as it was and with the Reds in another pennant race, I knew there was going to be no rush to try it again. I would have recommended holding off anyway, until we all had a chance to catch our breaths ... until the "Hometown Hubris" exhibit had come down.

A couple of weeks before the exhibit was scheduled to come down on the last day of September, Marty called my attention to an odd news item on the blog of a guy who lives in Cooperstown and writes about the Hall of Fame there. Seems they were having the opposite problem we were having. In the old days before the Inductions got to be so popular they had to be moved to the grounds of the high school on the outskirts of town, the ceremonies were held on the steps of the Hall of Fame Library in Cooperstown Park, which is adjacent to the Hall of Fame's main building. Nobody knew how or why but wild roses had started growing all along the Library building. They grew so fast and profusely that the groundskeepers had trouble controlling them. In frustration the head groundskeeper there ordered the bushes eradicated, but as fast as the gardeners could dig them up new bushes sprouted and bloomed.

When I called Brad Davis, my colleague at the Hall of Fame, to ask about the rose bushes, he was pretty nonchalant about the situation, describing it as little more than a nuisance that thankfully it wasn't his job to deal with. I let the silence between us linger a little longer than you would in a normal conversation, causing him to become a little suspicious.

"Why are you so interested in what we got growing up here in New York, John," he asked.

"I don't know. I guess because they're roses. I kind of have a thing for roses, you know? They're my favorite flower, and I'm intrigued anytime I hear something unusual about them."

There was an even longer silence then, and I imagined I could picture Brad sitting there debating whether or not he should keep talking.

"'Unusual', huh? I got something unusual for you. … If you promise to keep this under your hat. We don't need a lot of hoopla over something like this, and we certainly don't want to encourage more of this kind of thing."

I waited a few moments, and then said, "What? I promise. My lips are sealed."

"I can't even remember when this started now, but it's been going on for some time. … Every day somebody leaves a rose in the Museum. A single rose. Always in a different place. We don't know why, and we've never been able to catch the person or persons who are doing this. … I guess it's kind of a nice gesture, when you think about it, and it doesn't hurt anything, even though, on the other hand, you might think it's just as creepy as nice."

"Yeah, I can see it both ways," I said coolly, trying to disguise my intense interest in what Brad was telling me. "People think our jobs are pretty routine and totally predictable, huh? If they only knew."

I gave Brad a few moments to relax before casually probing into his business one more time. "Anything else weird ever happen at the Hall of Fame … that you're aware of," I said.

"Well, yes and no, because I don't think this really happened, but we had a part-time guard one time who claimed he kept seeing something weird in the museum when nobody but him was in the room."

"What happened to the guard?"

"We fired him. He had to be drinking on the job … or coming in wasted."

"What'd he claim to see?"

"A kid, carrying around a bat and a glove."

"What's so strange about that?"

"You don't understand. He was a kid who'd just disappear into thin air after a few moments."

"Did that guy need the job?" I asked.

"I can't remember. Maybe … but a lot of our part-timers just love baseball or they're retired and just like to be out of the house, away from the wife, or the husband, for that matter. You know how it is."

"Yeah, I do know how it is, Brad. Even so, if somebody else ever claims to see this kid you're talking about, you might want to make sure he doesn't really need the job before you let him go."

The Rose Garden remained a dead zone for the rest of that season. That didn't stop the rose petals from showing up on the stairs at some point every night after the Museum closed. If I didn't collect them at night or even see them before we went home, they'd be there waiting for us the next morning. I picked up every petal. By the time the last day of "Hometown Hubris" finally rolled around, I had a large, black Hefty garbage bag stuffed with rose petals. That morning, before we opened the doors to the public, I emptied that bag in the room that housed the exhibit and spread the petals around. The entire wood floor was covered by them, and as people began to walk into and out of the room, their shoes picked the petals up and carried them to other parts of the Museum, into the Gift Shop, and out onto the streets of Cincinnati.

The next spring, while the Reds were still in Arizona getting ready for the new season, we completely re-planted the Rose Garden a second time. After the harsh winter we'd just been through, with weeks on end of snow, freezing rain, bleak skies, and unending dirty slush in the streets, the carpet of red those rose bushes laid out next to the Museum was a beautiful sight indeed. As before, it was a two-day job, and when Charlie and his crew left for their suppers at the end of the second day the sun was going down again beyond the Roebling Suspension bridge over the Ohio. I told Marty to go on without me, that I had a report I needed to work on. I walked him to the front door, said "G'night, see you tomorrow," and then didn't even bother to lock the doors before heading back upstairs. I did read for a while … in Greg Rhodes' great book on Reds' Opening Days, just in case the media guys would ask me in a couple of weeks for some stuff that would help them with their reports on the new, upcoming Opening Day … until I couldn't sit still any longer. There was something drawing me to the stairs between the second and third floors. The rose petals again? I wondered.

I saw nothing on the stairs so I started to climb to the third floor. Halfway up I stopped to take another look down at the Garden, and there he was … the scruffy kid with the bat and glove, standing in the middle of beautiful new rose bushes. He was looking up at me, smiling a smile that revealed a gap between his two front teeth. As I raised my hand to wave at him, he tipped his cap … as smartly as any pro ballplayer I'd ever seen do it. Then he turned and seemed to melt away right into the bushes. Half a minute later, I realized I still had my hand in the air. I pulled it down and headed back to the office for my jacket. After setting the alarm and locking the front doors, I started the walk to the parking garage beneath Great

American Ballpark. I knew I'd never see the kid again. But the roses in the Rose Garden? … I knew they'd be there tomorrow, that we'd never have to re-plant them again.

# The Goat

Chucky Brown settled under the high fly ball hit to straightaway center field in Candlestick Park, thrice slapped his thigh with his gloved hand in the gesture that signaled to Yankee fans that Chucky had this one in his back pocket, reached up one-handed for the ball at precisely the right moment, caught the ball in his Rawlings Chucky Brown Gold Glove model, imagined the glory of tomorrow's headlines, and dropped it.

For a few more moments the seventh game of the World Series, which should have just ended, was still on.

The Yankees had taken a 1-0 lead in the top of the ninth on Brown's third hit of the Series, a wind-blown opposite field home run to right, and the Yankees great pitcher, Mel Martin, had retired the first two Giants in the bottom of the ninth before surrendering a bloop single to the third; but now the Giants runner, who had started from first base running at three quarters speed, was already around third base and would score easily to tie the score at 1-1. No questions about that. Despite his disappointment at having hit a routine fly ball, the batter, the Giants second baseman Roberto Sangria, had sprinted from home plate and was nearing second when his fly ball was dropped. Looking into center field he saw Chucky Brown reach down to pick up the ball and accidentally kick it towards the infield. With the third base coach waving him on wildly, Sangria decided to try to end the game right there. The Yankees shortstop, who had drifted into the outfield as soon as the fly had gone up, raced to intercept the ball rolling towards him. He picked it up in shallow left-center, whirled, and desperately fired the ball in the direction of home plate. It was a good effort, but the throw was a little short and up the line a bit. As soon as Sangria slid across home plate with the winning run, his teammates were there to mob him. Within seconds, the playing field was overrun by crazed fans, acting like characters in a Hieronymous Bosch painting come-to-life.

In anticipation of the possibility of such post-game bedlam, Yankees management had hired uniformed security guards, two per player, to assist their players off the diamond. The guards performed very capably, but even so, it took a good twenty minutes for all nine of the Yankees players on the field when the game ended to reach the visitors' clubhouse. Seven of them were no longer in possession of their ball caps, six had lost their gloves, and only the shin guard on his left leg remained to indicate that Stew Bragan had been catching.

As for Chucky Brown, he was so stunned by the last play of the World Series that the two security guards assigned to him had to literally lift him off the ground, one on each elbow, and carry him ten yards or so through the swarm of celebrating souvenir hunters before the center fielder's mind cleared and he began to move under his own power. Ironically, Chucky was the only Yankee to reach the clubhouse without being robbed of something.

By the time Chucky trudged into the Yankees' clubhouse, most of his teammates were already half dressed in their civilian clothes or were finishing their showers. Uniforms and towels were strewn about on the floor, and an interview platform stood, empty and useless, in the middle of the room. Topless soft drink coolers, full of expensive bottles of champagne packed in ice, lined two sides of the platform.

Nobody noticed Chucky as he walked over to his cubicle, and nobody said anything like, "Tough luck, Chucky," or "Hey, we'll get 'em tomorrow, kiddo." In fact, nobody was saying anything except the Yankees equipment manager who gave hurried, whispered directions to his two young assistants. Chucky decided not to shower; he knew his teammates wanted to get away from Candlestick Park as fast as possible, and he was with them there. Facing away from the middle of the room, he shed his uniform, wiped off with a clean towel, and began dressing.

A few moments later a badly dressed man with glasses, a beer belly, and a thick black beard, came over to Chucky's cubicle. It was Marshall James, the Yankees Public Relations Director, who at six feet four stood six inches taller than Chucky. "Chucky," he said, "I closed the clubhouse to the media. That makes me the second most unpopular guy in New York right now. You're gonna have to talk to 'em tomorrow though. I'll set up a news conference at the Stadium." Keeping his back to James, Chucky nodded.

Chucky tried to walk out of the clubhouse nonchalantly as part of a group of Yankees players, but the media guys, frustrated, frantic, and angry, were all over him. They shouted at him, jabbed microphones in his face, and blocked his path to the team bus.

"Chucky, did you choke?"

"What were you thinking when you dropped the ball?"

"Did you kick the ball on purpose out of anger?"

"Have you considered the repercussions of your double error?"

"Chucky, do you feel like killing yourself?"

Chucky crossed his forearms as if he were warding off vampires and charged through the media mob. A mini-cam guy on the left and a female reporter on the right were knocked on their asses. Both were trampled by their cohorts trying to keep up with the prey. As Chucky reached the safety of the team bus, he heard a Giants fan, hanging around to gloat, yell gleefully, "Brown, you stink!"

The charter flight back to New York seemed to take three days. Although some of the players began to talk quietly, and even though a low chuckle could occasionally be heard, a palpable gloom hung over the depressed team. Near the end of the flight, the captain spoke over the intercom: "Gentlemen, we've had a change in plans. We will be landing at Newark instead of LaGuardia. I hope you've had an enjoyable flight, and thank you for allowing us to serve you." What the captain didn't say but was already known throughout the cabin was that a full scale riot involving thousands of Yankees fans and hundreds of policemen had erupted at LaGuardia and spilled onto the tarmac scheduled for the charter's landing. Sitting by himself in the last row of the cabin, Chucky continued staring blankly at a magazine in his lap, but if he had looked up when the captain made his announcement he would have seen everyone in the cabin turn around in his seat to look at him.

The next morning, after being unable to reach Chucky by phone, Marshall James drove over to Chucky's condo in Manhattan. The condo manager, a short goateed Jew wearing navy slacks and a white turtleneck, let James into the spacious lobby of the building after James had held up to the glass entrance doors a leather writing pad embossed with the Yankees logo.

"How could he drop the ball?" the manager asked.

"What floor?" said James.

"My granddaughter could have caught that ball. Twelve. And then he had to go and kick it? Was the schmuck on drugs or something?"

James was already nearing the elevators when the manager called after him, "He's not there."

"What?"

"He's gone. He said to give you this."

James took the envelope, opened it, and read: "Sorry man. The heat is too hot. See you in Lauderdale next spring. Chuckles." James knew he was now in for serious abuse from the insatiable New York media, but in a way he didn't blame Brown for ducking out of the press conference. The newspaper headline writers had already had a field day:

"GOOD GRIEF, CHARLIE BROWN!"
"NOT SINCE MERKLE!"
"HITLER, STALIN, BROWN!"

The radio talk shows were worse. The callers were vicious enough on their own, but ratings-conscious hosts fanned the flames by soliciting suggestions on the best way to even the score with the dirty cur who had single-handedly cost the New York Yankees their first World Championship since 1978.

Driving his black Lexus to his ranch outside Chivo, Texas, Chucky heard on the radio that he'd been released by the Yankees. "This has nothing to do with the World Series," said a Yankees official. "We think our Triple A center fielder is ready, and he deserves a chance to show what he can do."

Chucky decided to spend the night at a Hilton outside Nashville, Tennessee, that had advertisements up and down the interstate for its huge, heated, guitar-shaped swimming pool. He paid cash and registered under a fake name, but the desk clerk recognized him and ducked into an office behind her to notify her boss. The manager, an ex-college football player with wide shoulders and a thick neck, came out of his office beaming. "Damn! It **is** him! Mr. Brown, on behalf of all Yankee haters everywhere, I want to shake your hand. Hey, everybody, look who's..." Chucky grabbed his valise and room key and sprinted for closing elevator doors. He locked and bolted the door to his room on the sixth floor, flopped on the double bed, and fell into a deep sleep.

He woke up around ten the next morning and called room service to order a huge breakfast. While waiting for his breakfast to arrive, he sat on the edge of his bed munching M&Ms from the "complimentary" snack bar in the room. Absentmindedly, he turned on the TV which was tuned to ESPN. Chucky saw an army of television camera crews camped out on both sides of some poor slob's long driveway and realized with horror that he recognized the sprawling adobe-style house in the background. He turned up the sound and heard: "... still waiting for World Series goat Chucky Brown to roost and face the music. Brown is rumored to be holed up in a hotel outside Nashville, Tennessee, but that report cannot be confirmed at this time. Stay tuned for an update on the

Chucky Brown situation every half hour." Chucky immediately dropped the bag of M&Ms and his plans for returning to the peace and quiet of home, grabbed up his car keys, and raced to his car in the parking lot. He drove to the airport, left his Lexus in long-term parking, picked up sunglasses and a Grand Old Opry cowboy hat at an overpriced gift shop, and bought a ticket for Billings, Montana. Chucky had planned to do some hunting in the off-season, and, with the way things were going, it seemed like a good idea to get started right away. Chucky rented a jeep at the Billings airport and then took out a week's rental on a cabin near the Yellowstone River. Still wearing his gift shop disguise, he drove to an outfitter's store, where he bought underwear, long johns, four flannel shirts, three pairs of jeans, two pairs of boots, a shotgun, plenty of ammo, and a week's worth of groceries. Just breathing the cool fresh air of Montana was a tonic for him, and he even began to feel a desire for some normal interaction with other human beings. He decided to have a few beers at Merle's Stop-Inn, about six miles from the cabin on the road to Billings. On the way there, Chucky thought it had been a good idea to come up to Montana. Hardly anybody up here even knows what happened in the World Series, he thought, and even if they do they don't give a shit.

The gravel crunched beneath the jeep's tires as Chucky pulled into Merle's parking lot. A phone booth stood next to the building, leaning away from it, and was illuminated by an arc lamp hanging off a blackened telephone pole. The arc lamp buzzed noisily, and huge moths fluttered around it. Chucky stepped inside the booth and dialed the number for his agent, Barry Price, in Waterbury, Connecticut.

"Hiya, Barry, guess who," said Chucky.

"Chucky, is that you?"

"Yeah, it's me, man."

"Where the hell are you, Chucky?" said the agent.

"I'm at Merle's Stop-Inn, 'bout to have me a couple of beers and talk huntin' with the local yokels."

"Merle's Stop-Inn? Where the hell … Never mind. Look, Chucky, we need to talk. The Yankees released you, you know."

"Yeah, I **know**, man. That's why I'm calling you. I'm spending money like there ain't no tomorrow. Can they do that, man? And they still gotta pay me, right, man?

"Yes, they can … you are released … and, yes, they still have to honor the remaining two years of your contract."

"Well, I guess you already been shopping around. Who wants me the most? And how much they offering?"

"Chucky, that's what I need to talk to you about."

"Yeah, who then? How much?"

"Chucky, nobody wants you."

"Nobody wants me?"

"Nobody in the American or National League."

"Damn. I don't know if I want to play in Japan. The money better be big, real big."

"They don't want you in Japan, either, Chucky."

"What in the hell…? Well, WHO THE HELL DOES WANT ME!?"

"Well, we've got a feeler from a team in Poland."

"POLAND!? Screw that, man … and screw you too. **SCREW EVERYBODY!!**" Chucky barged out of the phone booth, not even bothering to hang up the phone. A tiny voice came out of the receiver, saying, "Chucky, don't be hasty. I can still make … **we** can still make some money on this thing. Look at what Bob Uecker did. Chucky? … Chucky?"

Although there was a good crowd inside Merle's, Chucky had no problem finding a seat at the bar because everybody was out in the middle of the place dancing to the juke box. Chucky sipped his beer and tried to forget the sound of Barry Price's voice. He tried to focus on his plans for the next morning's hunting, but some new distraction was intruding into his thoughts. Chucky noticed the bartender, oblivious to his staring, smiling broadly as he did some sort of awkward dance while drying off a beer mug with a towel. The bartender then stood still, slapped his thigh three times with the back of his hand, intentionally dropped the beer mug, and took an exaggerated swipe at it with his right foot. At the same time, Chucky heard the crash of other mugs and glasses on the dance floor behind him. He turned around, saw the dancers completing kicks similar to the bartender's, and finally tuned in the song on the juke box that had been burrowing into his consciousness:

"One out to go in the seventh game.
Just a can of corn by any other name.
One catch to make, and it's glory and fame.
Instead you drop kick it, drive us all insane!

Hey, Joe, hey Joe, hey Joe,
So glad you didn't catch that show!
One thing's for sure
If you didn't know:
Chucky Brown ain't no Di-Mag-gio!

We're doin' the Chucky Shuffle!
Doin' the Chucky Shuffle …
Doin' the Chucky …"

Before he stormed out of the beer joint, Chucky threw his mug across the room. It smashed through the top of the juke box, rendering it instantly silent. After the startled cries of surprise and protest died down, somebody said, "What's his problem?"

The bartender said, "I don't know, but that boy's got a Major League arm on him."

Chucky Brown was at peace at last on this Nepalese national holiday. He was dressed in resplendent royal robes and was seated in the biggest, plushest chair he had ever sat in–it was a small throne actually–to the right of the King of Nepal. An interpreter sat between the King and Chucky. The King, his Queen on his left, the interpreter, and Chucky were all sitting on a raised dais outside the Imperial Palace, enjoying the parade passing before them down the narrow main boulevard of Katmandu. Both sides of the boulevard were packed with natives attired in colorful garb, and royal guardsmen dressed in elaborate uniforms and carrying lances rode by on horses and elephants. With the exception of a run-down old Mercedes which transported the King's generals, the entire scene was identical to the one which might have transpired a thousand years before.

The travel agent Chucky had hired to get him as far away from baseball as possible had certainly known what she was doing in sending him to the Himalayas, as Chucky had not even thought about the American national pastime for the past week. The trip had not only deposited Chucky outside the sphere of baseball, but it also had managed to soothe his battered ego in a most memorable way. Somehow, the travel agent had gotten Chucky an audience with the King of Nepal. Impressed by Chucky's wealth and a humility uncharacteristic of Westerners, the King had taken a liking to Brown and insisted that he serve as His Highness' right-hand man in the holiday ceremonies. As there was only one simple duty involved, the appointment was almost entirely honorary, and Chucky felt the honor deeply.

At the conclusion of the parade, the Queen reached into a basket and pulled out a very large, beautifully decorated egg. The sacred egg was to be carried to a shrine in the highest reaches of the mountains, with its successful journey there supposedly ensuring prosperity in the coming year for everyone in the kingdom. Over the centuries the delicate egg had not received even the slightest crack on its many tortuous journeys. A royal carriage now waited for the egg on the boulevard below the dais. Chucky's crucial moment as the King's right-hand man had arrived. He stood, walked over to the Queen, and bowed deeply. He took the egg from her carefully, and holding it reverently before him, proceeded down the steps of the dais.

What happened next was all too predictable. It shattered Chucky's short-lived contentment and obliterated his blessed anonymity. And it happened right at the moment the tourist with the camera and the New York Yankees' ball cap shouted, "Holy shit! It's that butter-fingered son of a bitch, Chucky Brown!"

# The Greatest Story Never Told

I write with the full knowledge that the highest point of my professional career has just passed me by, remaining unattained, with my complete if silent complicity. As a Christian, as a fair-minded citizen of the United States, indeed, as a human being concerned with the welfare of my fellow man, I am willingly leaving unwritten–except in the pages of my private journal–the greatest story any young sports reporter could ever hope to encounter. My fate, I feel, is thus akin to that of the photographer who misses the greatest picture of his life, a Pulitzer winner, because of a moment's inattention, to the athlete who falls short of greatness because of injury, to the wife who realizes she loved most the man she loved first and declined to marry.

Yet, it is not myself and this renounced opportunity for advancing my career that I regret though my renunciation does not nullify my awareness of the sensationalist nature of the story. Rather, it is the unfortunate string of recent events connected with the story, one of the most tragic in American history, that I regret and the circumstances surrounding them that forbid me from fulfilling my professional journalistic duties as I normally would.

Exactly why I am filing this story within these pages (and my memory) instead of with my paper will become apparent soon enough to anyone (whoever you are) who eventually reads this journal, sometime in the distant future (if at all), but suffice it to say at this point that there is no question in my mind that by spiking this story I am following an eminently higher principle than any of those which would compel the editors of many papers to run the story, including that of "the public's right to know," so much in vogue among the avant-garde in the business, among whose number I count many of my superiors at the *Courier-Journal*.

Some of my colleagues would doubtlessly call me a fool if they were privy to my self-muzzling, but I care not a fig for their opinion. I could no more publish a story that would jeopardize someone's personal safety than a man could fly to the moon. And I shudder to think what might happen, given the events of the last few days, were the story I am about to commit to this journal to become public and accessible to those who would use it (twisting it and exaggerating it) to re-ignite the shocking fires of violence and racial hatred in America that have only just begun to be doused. The National Guards in the South have stopped the lynchings, and the rioting in New York

... Washington ... St. Louis ... Los Angeles and elsewhere has been brought under control, but confusion, anger, disappointment, fear, mistrust, and plain ugly prejudice remain mixed in a powder keg of emotion with a dangerously short fuse called American Society, needing only the smallest spark to set off an explosion of bloodshed more terrible than the one that occurred after Pee Wee Reese was shot; and I will not publish the story that would most certainly be that spark.

I mention the shooting of Pee Wee Reese, rather than the death of Cotton Shaw, because the shooting WAS the precipitous event. The crowd at Sportsman Park was stunned and horrified when it realized that Shaw was dead, but none of the fans made a sound or moved a muscle (according to wire reports) until the rifle shot rang out moments later and Reese, standing next to Robinson, fell over like a duck in a shooting gallery. That's when all hell broke loose. Somehow, seeing Reese go down transformed that mute and paralyzed crowd of baseball fans into an angry vengeful mob that came pouring out of the grandstands in a frenzy. The shooting released some pent-up ugliness in the St. Louis fans and in the American people across the country. But all this, including the ensuing race-riot at Sportsman Park that spilled out into the St. Louis streets, is well known now. It's time for me to begin my story.

Yesterday (Thursday) being a travel day, I was riding with the Colonels on our way to Kansas City for a four game series with the Blues. The Colonels had just completed a very successful home stand (9-3) which put Louisville on top of the American Association standings for the first time in this 1947 season, and the fellows were in great spirits, brimming with confidence and enjoying the feeling of being a first-place ball club.

To my surprise the team had not been terribly upset when news of Sunday's horrible events in St. Louis was released to them while they were noisily celebrating in the clubhouse their just-completed doubleheader sweep over Minneapolis. Most of the Colonels expressed some initial distress and repugnance at what had happened, but none of them seemed to be deeply disturbed, and after it had quieted down for a few moments the celebration went on as before.

I was terribly upset, both at the news and at this callous display of indifference toward what the *New York Times* the next day called "nothing less than an immense national tragedy." Bob Barnes, my avuncular colleague over at the *Standard*, sensed my feelings and told me not to be too hard on the Colonels. He said the Colonels concentrated so hard on their own struggles to do well and to get to the majors (some of them have been stuck in the minors for close to ten years) that they have by necessity developed one-track minds and the ability to block out anything that distracts them from reaching their goal. Concepts such as civil rights, equal opportunity, and a just society are as foreign to them as the works of Plato or Aristotle. The Colonels are so wrapped up in their own world that if Jackie Robinson represented anything to them he represented new competition, another obstacle for them to climb over, which is the last thing they feel they need. And to be honest about it, Big Bob said, although they aren't happy it happened the way it did, they probably aren't unhappy that Robinson didn't make it and bring in a bunch more coloreds after him.

That night I thought a lot about what Bob had said. Was Bob being more understanding than I am about these men, who are after all uneducated, limited, and desperate under the facade of heroism; or was he revealing a side of himself as insensitive, irresponsible, and prejudiced as the Colonels themselves? I finally decided, after 7 or 8 beers, that what he said made a lot of sense, but I still couldn't accept it.

There hadn't been any trouble at the Louisville ballpark that day. The Colonels organization had had the good sense to employ a news blackout at the ballpark, and their sagacity surely prevented the occurrence of bloody confrontations there. Unfortunately, however, it was not possible for the city of Louisville to employ a similar blackout and that night there were racial incidents all over the city.

I am not being heartless when I say that *only* two of our Negroes were killed in the violence that night; it is just an admission to the horrifying fact that many more than two were killed that night in other cities around the country. While I was outraged at the death of the two, I am realistic enough to realize that it could have been much worse, especially considering the fact that Pee Wee Reese is Louisville's favorite son. People were distraught over Reese's condition, with his life hanging in the balance, but it wasn't just the whites. Louisville's Negroes are proud of Reese too, and when their leaders like the Reverend Clay went on the radio to express their sorrow and to pray for Pee Wee's survival, the whites of good will knew, if they had doubted it before, that Louisville's Negroes are good people. Still, here as elsewhere, the news of the shooting brought out the worst in the worst, and to their everlasting shame the violently disposed in Louisville used their loyalty to Reese as a misguided excuse for their despicable actions, setting fires to three Negro schools (all three burned to the ground) and to a couple of dozen houses in the Negro neighborhoods. All night I stood on the balcony outside the bedroom of my apartment and watched the bright yellow flames licking the black night sky, and the bells of the city's fire engines rang in my ears continuously, and for the first time in my life I was ashamed of the city in which I'd been born. Last Sunday night no one slept in Louisville. Last Sunday night no one slept in America.

Unless, of course, it was the Louisville Colonels baseball club. Like a poisonous cloud, racial tension still hangs in the air, and every day the government restricts the freedom of the Negro and erects more barriers to keep the races apart, all in the name of protecting the Negro (instead of vigorously prosecuting the whites who commit acts of violence and terror against him); yet the Colonels are as happy as larks and promise to continue that way as long as they kept winning. They are a remarkably imperturbable bunch, so much so that yesterday on the train their insouciance simply became too much for me to endure any longer.

I had no desire to join their card games or their conversations and wanted nothing so much as to get as far away from them as possible. I was still angry with them and wanted to dissociate myself from their attitude. I got up and walked out of the club car they had taken over and headed towards the rear of the train. I gave no thought as to where I was going, but as I passed through the fourth or fifth car I suddenly got an appealing idea. I decided I would join the passengers in the Negro car at the end of the train. It would be a protest (though one without much of an impact on anything but my own psyche) and a gesture of friendship both. I would be sure to sit by a window so that when we pulled into stations along our route, people would notice a white man sitting in the Negro car as if it were the most natural thing in the world to do, and maybe it would give them ideas too, make them think, for God's sake.

None of the other passengers paid me any attention, and the U.S. Army guards at the front of the Negro car (ordered there on all trains to keep order and discourage confrontations) merely nodded an acknowledgment. There weren't more than a dozen Negroes in the whole car, most of them women and children, all occupying seats toward the front of the car. There was one man with a seat in the middle on the right-hand side of the aisle, but he was sleeping, pressed up against the side of the car with a straw hat pulled down over his face to keep the morning daylight out of it. The other man in the car was a friendly-looking sort near the rear, in an aisle seat, wide awake and actually smiling broadly as he watched me walk towards him.

I smiled at him, said, "Good morning," and pulled into the aisle seat directly opposite him (it would have been presumptuous for me to have requested the window seat next to him). I don't know what I'd have said if he had asked me why I was sitting in the car for coloreds, but he never asked. He didn't bring up any of the troubles afflicting our nation and his race, nor did I. We discussed train travel, the weather, tobacco farming, and his relatives. His sister was getting married in St. Louis, and he was on his way to the wedding. Our conversation was so relaxed and relaxing I was sorry to see him get off the train.

Shortly after we left St. Louis was when a very odd thing occurred. We had just gotten rolling good when all of a sudden I and all the other passengers were thrown forward practically out of our seats when the train abruptly stopped. Actually, the train never completely stopped moving, but it slowed down so drastically that it seemed as if it had completely stopped.

I estimated that we were about 20 miles west of St. Louis. From my aisle seat I could see only fields of corn and distant farmhouses, nothing that would have explained the need for the braking. I thought that maybe a loose cow had wandered onto the tracks in front of the engine.

I moved over into the window seat and noticed already behind us (as we continued moving down the line) a country road crossing (no signal arm) and a blue sedan pulled up to the tracks. Two men stood there watching us move away; one on the driver's side of the car, the other on the passenger side, both with one foot still resting on the floor of the car. For a second I concluded that we had nearly collided with that sedan, but then I reconsidered. The engineer had not sounded the train's whistle as a warning (as he'd have done even for a cow), and the men standing by the auto didn't look the least bit angry and shaken up as they surely would have had they just narrowly avoided a certain death.

Then, turning away from the window, I was astonished to see two men, one Negro and one white, being ushered into the car by the conductor. Had they just boarded the train? It certainly seemed so; both carried small grips and quickly, almost furtively, scanned the car with a manner that indicated they were looking over new surroundings.

The white man appeared to be in his mid-forties and was of medium build, but he carried himself like an athlete (after hanging around sports all my life I can spot an athlete when I see one) and looked like he was still in pretty good shape. When the man spotted me, he stiffened in surprise almost imperceptively, as if he caught himself, but I did notice.

The Negro was older. He walked with a cane; and though he wore a natty fedora pulled down over his forehead, patches around his temples where his hair had turned white revealed his age.

The conductor left the car, and as the two men came down the aisle, the Negro moving slowly in front of the white man, something that didn't figure happened, again. For the second time, the train lurched violently. Evidently, the engineers were trying to quickly get the train back up to speed, and everyone was pitched forward again. The white man lost his balance and almost fell into a seat behind himself. However, the Negro, the one with the cane, hardly faltered at all. With the adroitness of a cat he maintained his balance by assuming with astonishing quickness a stance that resembled nothing so much as it resembled an infielder's ready position: knees bent, feet spread, his arms held out away from his sides. It was an amazing reaction for such an old man, too amazing really, and it made me suspicious. Actually, I should say it made me more suspicious because once I decided that the two men had indeed boarded back at that country crossroad,

I realized that they had had to literally jump aboard a moving train! Hardly a normal procedure for anybody, much less for an old man with a cane and especially when a major station on the line was only some 20 miles to the east back in St. Louis.

The Negro took a window seat on the left about hallway down the car. After recovering, the white man took the aisle seat in the row behind the Negro. Again, a curious thing because although they didn't sit together in the same row, I felt certain that, for whatever reason, they were traveling together.

The Negro immediately tilted his seat back and turned his head to the side to take a nap. The white man opened a newspaper, but before he began to read he turned his head and peered at me, as if checking to make sure I was still sitting in my seat. I nodded to him in a friendly way, but he ignored the gesture and turned to bury his face in his newspaper.

By this time I was monumentally intrigued by the whole curious situation, and having been a reporter for five years now I felt bold enough and competent enough, and obligated in a way, to find out what was going on. I didn't really have a plan of any kind, but I moved up to the aisle seat opposite the white man and sat down.

Although the man was surely aware of my presence, he ignored me. It was then that I noticed two more things that finally enabled me, in a rush of insight, to put two and two together.

From holding the newspaper out wide, the man's right hand was conspicuously extended outwards toward the aisle, and I couldn't help but notice how crooked and big-knuckled his long fingers were. The throwing hand of an old catcher, I thought. And then I noticed the ring. I could hardly believe it, but there was no mistaking such a ring ... gold, with a big blue stone, the words "BROOKLYN DODGERS" circled around the stone in block letters, and the year "1941" embossed on the right side of the shank. It was a World Series ring, there was no doubt of that; and unless I missed my guess, the owner of the ring was Clyde Sukeforth, the Dodger coach (and former catcher and scout), and the Negro in the seat in front of him was none other than Jackie Robinson, white hair and cane or no white hair and cane.

I was stunned and excited, but I could still think clearly. A lot of things now started to add up. Robinson had not returned to Brooklyn on Monday as the papers had reported. He had stayed right in St. Louis all the time. No wonder none of the New York papers had been able to find him at his apartment and interview him. And Sukeforth, whose absence had been noticed and attributed to a death in his family, had not been to any funeral but had been chaperoning Robinson. And, now, the mysterious boarding outside St. Louis made sense too. Branch Rickey's hand was all over the situation. Rickey felt that Robinson's life was still in danger, and he wasn't taking any chances. He had assigned one of the most trusted people in his entire organization to chaperone Robinson, and he had arranged for the train to make a special, secret stop just to pick them up in the middle of nowhere so that Robinson would not be exposed to the public.

I took a deep breath and asked the man across from me, "Say, how'd the Dodgers do yesterday?" The man was reading the sports page, but I felt certain he didn't need to in order to keep up with the goings-on of the Brooklyn club.

Without so much as a rustle or a tremble of the papers, the man replied, "Lost again ... four to three in ten innings." The Dodgers had lost three in a row to the Reds since the game in St. Louis on Sunday had been interrupted, and they lost yesterday too.

"Who's pitching for Brooklyn this afternoon?" I asked.

"Taylor."

"How do you know that?" I asked. "The papers say Taylor OR Gregg."

Now, if they hadn't been before, the man's own suspicions were fully raised. He lowered his paper and turned to look at me carefully. I extended my hand towards him and said, "Mr. Sukeforth, my name is Percy Adams. I'm with the *Louisville Courier-Journal*, and I'm very pleased to meet you ... and your companion." Saying this, I shifted my eyes in the direction of Jackie Robinson sitting in front of Sukeforth.

Sukeforth ignored my outstretched hand, but he knew he had been found out. Hardly opening his mouth, he quietly expelled a foul oath before addressing me in earnest.

"Listen, Mr. Adams, I don't know why you're here—there weren't supposed to be any whites in this car, especially not any goddamned reporters—or how you knew we were getting on this train, but you've got to forget all about this. This man's life may still be in danger, and if you go blabbing about him in your paper and it gets picked up ..."

Sukeforth never finished because there suddenly was Robinson, leaning in towards me, ordering me to move over. As ordered, I moved into the window seat, and Robinson took my vacated seat on the aisle, opposite Sukeforth. Sukeforth started warning Robinson not to talk to me, but Jackie told him that now they didn't have any choice.

"Besides," Robinson said turning to me and fixing me with a withering glare, "this man knows what's at stake. I think we can trust him to keep our meeting and whatever we say here in the strictest of confidences."

The statement was more like a question or a challenge even, and I swore to them both with as much sincerity for Robinson's predicament as I could express that they could indeed trust me to keep our meeting secret.

Sukeforth mumbled something about Mr. Rickey while Robinson stared at me as intently as if I were a pitcher he'd never faced before.

I studied Robinson right back, remarking to myself how handsome he was, with his noble features, and the glossiness of his ebony skin. At a distance the white hair made him look aged, but up close one could see that his eyes were clear,

"Well, what do you want to know?" he finally asked.

I wanted to know everything, of course, but I was so excited I didn't have the presence of mind any longer to say, "Start at the beginning," but in retrospect I guess for him to have really started at the beginning he would have had to go back a lot farther than the start of Sunday's game or even the start of the season, maybe all the way back to his birth, or his daddy's birth or *his* daddy's birth.

At any rate, while I stammered about my horror and outrage at the events of the last few days, he cut me off and started in right at the crux of the matter.

"I'm not sorry for what I did to Cotton Shaw," he said. I guess I looked a bit stunned because he said, "Did you think I would be sorry?"

"I guess I thought … I mean, I …"

"I didn't mean to kill him, and I regret that he died, but not for his sake because Shaw was one mean no-good son-of-a-bitch. What I regret is all the bloodshed that's happened and all the misery it's brought down on my people. I didn't mean to kill him, but I did mean to hurt him. I wanted to hurt him bad too. I got that bunt down perfect, right on the first base line, so he had to field it.

I was going for his shoulder. I wanted to fuck it up good so his career'd be over, so he'd never be able to try to bean me again.

"I got to him when he was bent over, but instead of starting to straighten up to throw to first or to tag me, he moved into me like he was trying to tackle me. He brought his head around, and my knee popped him right here … right in the temple. That fucker got his head crushed."

"You're sure Shaw had been throwing at you? I mean really trying to hit you and not just brush you back?"

"Shit, man, I guess I know the difference by now. Who do you think's leading the league in getting hit? And it'd be three or four times as high as it is if it weren't for my reflexes. Shaw was fast, he could throw HARD, but nobody's fast enough to hit me in the head. Still, that don't mean it didn't make me mad when they tried to bean me. … Shaw wasn't just trying to brush me back. He tried to kill me."

"Well, I admit that Shaw was a mean one and that it was pretty dirty for him to try to intimidate you that way, but I can't believe he was really trying to … murder you."

Robinson looked past me and gazed out the window for a few moments as if he'd forgotten I was there. I squirmed nervously in my seat, as it was very uncomfortable to sit there in silence, knowing everything this man had been through, feeling powerless to help him any, and wondering what he was thinking and what was the right or wrong thing to say to him.

"It wasn't a matter of intimidation anymore. They'd all tried that already, all season, all over the league. The name calling, the spikings, the brush backs, the insults, the threats. I stood up to all that. No sir, Shaw was trying to take it a step further.

"Nobody knows about this. The Dodgers didn't want this getting in the papers, figuring it might encourage more of the same. The day before, on Saturday, the Cardinals were riding me all game long. The usual stuff: 'Hey, porter, carry my bags! Hey, boy, shine these shoes!' But then in the ninth inning Shaw started saying something kinda queer: 'Hey, Robinson, no smokin' in bed! Smokin' in bed'll kill ya, Robinson!' I thought he'd finally gone crazy listening to himself rant and rave all day. That night I found out otherwise. When I went to my room at the Royale, the Negro hotel, there it was, right in my bed, a charred cross, ten feet tall. All right, I thought, if that's how it's gonna be. I wasn't scared. I was outraged. But I promised myself, just like I'd promised Mr. Rickey, I wasn't going to start nothing. And I didn't. Shaw brought that thing on himself. I played it hard and tough, that's all. That son-of-a-bitch just happened to get exactly what he deserved."

"God, that's outrageous! Did you notify the police, Commissioner Chandler?"

"It wouldn't have done any good. We couldn't prove who did it. When I went down to the lobby to get a new room, I could see the fear in everybody's eyes. They saw that cross being brought in, but they'd been threatened not to say anything, and I didn't see any use in scaring them further or endangering them with a police investigation. I didn't ask any questions about it. Just said I wanted a new room. Besides, even though Shaw probably didn't do it himself, he knew about it, was probably behind it. That's all that mattered."

"And you knew Shaw would be pitching the next day."

"Yep. But that wasn't nothing to worry about. I always hit Shaw good, even when he was throwing at me. If you remember, after he hit me in the leg in the first inning. I got two doubles off him before I bunted in the seventh. There was also this."

Robinson reached inside his coat and withdrew a folded-up piece of lined paper, the kind kids use in school. He handed it to me. I unfolded it and read the following, printed in a crude hand, in pencil:

*dear nigger,*

*if you go on that field tomorrow you will be shot. this is no lie. dont*

*do it nigger or you will pay with your life, you ben warned.*

"The desk clerk at the hotel handed that to me when I went down to get a new room," Robinson said. "That wasn't the first death threat I got, but that's something you never get used to. We didn't know if there was any connection between the letter and the cross. ... It's possible there wasn't ... but coming so close together made them both seem more serious."

"You mean to tell me Shotton and Rickey let you go out there after this direct threat?"

"They couldn't stop me. After all I had already gone through and put up with, nothing was going to keep me out of the lineup. If I was good enough, I had a right to be there, and I've proven I deserve my place in the Dodger lineup. Besides, I didn't have just myself to think about. America is just a jungle for the Negro, thick with briars to cut him and snares to trip him. Every time I went out on that field I cleared some more path through that jungle. I wanted to keep moving through that jungle. I didn't want to stop for anything. I felt like as long as I kept moving forward, that path behind me stayed open, clear, but as soon as I stopped the jungle would start growing over it again."

I was overcome with emotions. I was angry, horrified, embarrassed, ashamed, sorrowful. I felt so bad for this man and for everything he had endured and for everything he would have to endure in the future, but above all I admired him for his courage.

"I know this doesn't mean much to you now, Jackie, but I have to tell you how much I admire you for your courage," I said. It was an eerie feeling talking to a man who had knowingly attended his own execution and survived. "It's a gruesome thought, but if that rifleman had been a better shot ..."

"Oh, he was a good shot all right. Damn good. I don't think he would have missed me if Pee Wee Reese hadn't got in his way. You see, I wanted to see how Shaw was, but as soon as it looked like he was hurt bad, Pee Wee was trying to get me off the field, the whole time trying to keep himself between me and the stands. That Pee Wee ..."

And here Robinson's voice faltered, grew even a little higher pitched, and I could see his eyes tear. He blinked back the tears and cleared his throat. Then a slight smile brightened his face again.

"You know what Reese told me before the game? We were warming up in front of the dugout, me and him standing next to each other. He looked at me real serious and said, 'Hey, Jack, move over some, will ya, about three or four steps.' 'Why, Pee Wee?' I said. He says, "Cause that guy who sent the letter might be a bad shot!' We had a good laugh over that. And then this morning when Pee Wee finally came to, he looked at me and smiled. Then he whispered, 'Jack ... I told you that guy might be a lousy shot.'"

"You saw him? Pee Wee's going to be okay then?"

"Yes."

"You were there when he regained consciousness .... You've been in St. Louis all this time to stay with Reese, haven't you?"

"Yes. I wouldn't be leaving unless I knew he was going to be all right."

"Well, how did you get in and out of the hospital without being seen?"

"I didn't. I stayed in the next room, and our rooms were connected. The Dodgers arranged it."

"Oh, I'm so glad about Pee Wee. Is he going to be able to play again? Did the doctors say?"

"Nobody even asked. First things first. He's got to fully recover first before he worries about playing major league ball again. But he's finished for the year, that's certain."

"And what about you, Jackie, are you finished too?" It may seem like a cruel question, but it was one I had to ask. Of all the questions which have been raging through America since Sunday's events, the one causing the most heated debate in the papers and on the streets and most likely in the private inner sanctums of the baseball establishment too has been what should be done about Jackie Robinson.

The worst bigots are still calling (absurdly) for Robinson to be arrested for murder. Other people, less bigoted but only slightly more enlightened, want Robinson banned from baseball for life and other blacks barred from ever entering baseball in the future. With convoluted logic these people blame Robinson (and Rickey too) for the Reese shooting and see the shooting as proof positive that the races absolutely cannot mix.

Officially, Commissioner Chandler has "temporarily" suspended Robinson "for his own protection and welfare." The Dodgers quietly filed a protest, essentially in order to go on record as supporting Robinson, because although they consider him blameless, they obviously agree that under the circumstances it is impossible for the man to continue playing.

Despite constant badgering from the press, Chandler refuses to specify how long Robinson's temporary suspension will remain in effect. Nevertheless, a consensus is already forming that, despite whatever is decreed, Robinson will never play in the major leagues again.

Robinson's face clouded over at the question, and it was several moments before he answered.

"Mr. Rickey wanted to be honest with me. He always has been. He said he didn't know what would happen with me and baseball, but that the situation was very bad. He's promised to do whatever he can do, but as you know, Mr. Rickey's almost as unpopular right now as I am. He wants me to stay in shape and work out every day at home in California, but he said there's a good chance I won't be able to play anymore this season. Mr. Rickey's already making arrangements for me to play winter ball in South America, but after that .... We just don't know." He studied me carefully as he spoke, as if trying to read my thoughts, my reaction to his answer, in my face. I've never felt so strongly before the force of a person's gaze, and it seemed as if he could actually penetrate my mind. I feared the worst for him and for his race, and he spoke to my fears.

"I know it may be all over for me, but you'll never hear me crying about poor little Jackie Robinson. They can keep me out of their game if they want to, but I know now that I'm as good as any white ball player. They know that too, America knows it, and they can't take that away from me.

"But I grieve … I grieve for my black-skinned brothers and sisters. … I've failed them. I did my best. … I took so much abuse and turned the other cheek, but I always played hard and fought hard to prove myself and my race. I was only defending myself when I bunted against Shaw. My teammates knew what I was doing, and they approved. They hated Shaw as much as I did. But that doesn't make any difference now."

As Robinson finished, he sounded very tired, and he seemed (with the lines in his face and the white hair around his temples) to become an old man again. I too felt completely drained, and I wanted a respite from the intensity generated by the tortured soul of this great, tragic man. Robinson gave me a "That's it" look, got up, and returned to his original seat. I thanked him for his time and candor, wished him well, and again assured him and Sukeforth of my absolute trustworthiness. Robinson went to sleep immediately. As I stood up ready to return to my place among the Colonels, I recommended to

Sukeforth that Robinson continue to dye his hair white as the disguise had certainly helped fool me, if only temporarily.

Sukeforth's reply sent me on my way with one final shock. "He's not coloring his hair white. ... He's just not coloring it black anymore to hide the white."

As I walked through the cars towards the front of the train I thought, "If I am underestimating the ordeal he faces in the future as much as I have underestimated the ordeal he has already gone through, then God help Jackie Robinson." A moment later I added, "And God help us all."

# A Whole Lot of Bar-B-Q

The day I become a mul-tie-millionaire I knew right away what I wanted to do with the money. It took me bout ten seconds to answer Sis, my older siblin' whose real name is Ada Sarah, when she says, "Fargo, what you planning on doin' with your half of the in-hare-tance?"

"Sis," says I, "I'm gonna buy me a pro baseball team."

Ever since I hurt my pitchin' arm at Walters State Junior College freshman year, a coupla years after Daddy moved us from North Dakota once Momma died, I been dreaming of getting to the majors some other way, and since I wasn't never no kind of hitter and woulda never umpire even if you paid me, I figgered being a owner was the way to go. I don't never think I ever had a swelled head, even when I owned the best fastball in this part of Tennessee, but for some reason I wanted people to know I was in pro ball and to be jealous of me for being in it, just like I envied ever body who was in pro ball even though I dint really know nobody personal-like who was in pro ball, what with me working at the check-in desk at the Cookeville Motor Lodge. Right before Daddy hit it big I was gonna start lookin' into how to go bout getting myself hired by a pro team, and then I was gonna work my way up from the bottom of the barrel. But after Daddy died … well, that changed ever thang. Now, I wasn't dumb enough to think that I was gonna buy the New York Yankees right out from under Mr. Steinberger's nose, but I figgered my thirteen and a half millions of Lotto dough would be plenty to pick up some other major league team not so high and mighty as the Yankees, like the Cincinnata Redlegs or maybe them lousy Pirates out of Pixburg, P-A. Turns out though after I made a few polite inquiries that Cincinnata and Pixburg was outta my league, money-wise. Turns out, in fact, that my stash could not even buy the Padres or the Royals, teams that nobody even knows who they play for.

Before Daddy died he had started spending some of his winnin's on hisself, which nobody in his right mind coulda said he had no right to do. After all, he was the one who picked the Pick Six numbers 'sactly right, wasn't he? First thing he did was buy hisself a brand new cherry Cadillac from Cookeville Chevrolet. It only cost him twenty-four grand 'cause he traded in his semi which he wasn't gonna be driving all over kingdom come no more. Then he bought Fred's Bar-B-Q rest-a-ront 'cause it's better than KFC, Sonic, and any of the other good rest-a-ronts in Putnam County. Daddy loved ever item on the menu at Fred's. He dint want to work there or manage the place. He jest wanted to be able to go in there and eat whatever he wanted ever day and then walk out without paying, like he owned the place. He paid $12,500 for the joint and he hired Fred to stay on as the cook and manager for $30,000 per year, which was a lot more than Fred ever made being the owner. Daddy also said Fred could keep on his wife Jo-Ann and their daughter Samantha JoAnn and even give them a dollar and a quarter raise per hour.

Ever body knows that when you buy a rest-a-ront you have to have a GRAND OPENING UNDER NEW MGMT party, so Daddy had one one Friday night after he put a ½ Off coupon on ever item on the menu in the paper. A course the place was packed that night like a pig farmer's jaw with Redman, and Daddy was in his glory. All night he was eatin' corn on the cob, thick ole steak fries, cole slaw and ice tea sweeter than cotton candy, and the best bar-b-q in the state of Tennessee. Heck, I might as well go ahead and say it … the best bar-b-q in the whole dang South! Fred really outdid hisself with the cooking, and Jo-Ann and Sam JoAnn keep the food piled high on Daddy's paper plate. Around nine a clock he loosened his belt, bent over, and started groaning. He was sweating like he just come out of the shower and his face turned a blotchy red color. Jo-Ann gave Daddy some pink Pep-two-bismal and then she and Fred and me helped him out to his new green Cadillac in the parking lot so he could go on home to bed, but he never made it. They found him bout two hours later parked on the side of 42, dead. They said his appendix busted before he could drive hisself to the hospital, but I'm not sure to this day that it wasn't stomach ache. A man just cain't eat the way Daddy did that night and not 'spect some consequence.

After the funeral we had a little eat-together at Fred's again, nothing big, just the family and some of the close family friends. That's when Sis ast me what was I gonna do with my half of the money. When I ast her, she said she was gonna give a million to the 4th Baptist Congregation of Cookeville and put the rest in the bank for a rainy day. A month later she got married to Mr. Jessie Blackstone, the Congregation preacher and the lawyer who read Daddy's will and told us, official-like, we was both rich now. And now Sis wasn't a Miller no more but a Blackstone, jest like that.

After I got nowheres fast with the big league teams, I ast Jessie what should I do now about my dream, and he says, "Well, Fargo, I reckon you oughter still go after your dream jest like Ada Sarah wants to follow her dream of making Fred's Bar-B-Q into a national franchise operation. If you ain't got enough jangle in your pocket to suit the big boys, jest buy yourself some overalls that fit your budget better. Last I heard they got baseball in Memphis and Knoxville. Nashville too, I'm purty sure." Those were sweet words to my eardrums, that's for sure, but wouldn't you know it? After I made polite inquiries again, 'pears none of them teams was for sale.

Now all my money wasn't burning no hole in my pocket, but truth be tole I jest could not get being a owner of a pro baseball team out of my skull. That's what I was mulling over one day at Fred's whilst I dawdled over a plate of pulled pork and sipped on a big ole sweet tea when Bobby Hater, my old high school catcher, come in and set down acrosst the table. "Fargo," he says, "you look like a fella who is moonstruck over some purty girl who ain't paying him the time of day, even though we both knows you could have jest bout any girl in the county now."

"Hey, Bobby," says I. "You are 'sactly right. That's jest how I feel." Bobby always could read me like a comic book, which come in real handy when we was playing high school ball together. A pitcher and his catcher need to be what they call simpatico to do they best.

"Who's the girl then," he says. Bobby's hair line was pulling back like the North at Chickamauga, and he done put on a few more pounds around the middle to scale him up to bout 220, but other than that he looked like he could still squat down and catch a doubleheader in the middle of July, no problem.

"Ain't no girl," says I. "It's pro ball. I cain't find no team to be the owner of."

"Shoot. That shouldn't be no harder to fix than the mirror in a pickup. You jest put a ad in the paper."

"You mean in the *Cookeville Commerce*?" I says, already rising out of my funk.

"No, you knucklehead. In the *Baseball 'merica* paper that comes out of Carolina. Ever body who's any body in pro ball and college ball and minor league ball, they read that paper ever day, cover to cover."

Leave it to good ole Bobby Hater to know jest what pitch to throw in ever situation.

When the paper come out with my solicitation in it, the phone start ringing off the hook. That's the good part. The bad part is the teams was all in places nobody ever heard of like Kalamazoo or someplace in Canada for god's sake, or they was asking for more than thirteen and a half millions. A lot more. 'Course I knew where they was another thirteen and a half millions, but I never borrowed no money from my sister before and I dint want to start now that we was both rich. Besides, Sis and Jess was getting purty serious about the bar-b-q bidness and they done already opened a new Fred's in Crossville. In fact, they ast me did I want to come on board with them, and a course I had to politely dee-cline 'cause being a pro baseball team owner was jest not out of my system yet.

I still dint know what to do next until one day a man called me name of Burton. Burton was his first name. Last name of Terry. I know it seems like his parents named him backwards but that's what he had to go by. Anyway, Burton says, "Mr. Miller, jest how bad are you looking to get into pro baseball?"

"Purty bad, Mr. Terry, purty bad," I says. I dint see no purpose in being coy bout nut-in.

"Well," says he, "have you ever thought about Indy ball?"

Now if owning a team in Canada had no appeal for me, why would I even consider going all the way to India half way cross the ocean. I thought they dint have baseball over there no way. Figured they was all cricket players or soccer players or some such.

"No, no, not 'India,' says Burton. " 'Independent' baseball. You're not affiliated with the major leagues is all, but you're still pro."

Well, I had no idea, but it sounded fine to me. Pro is pro. And that's not all. Come to find out, 'cording to Mr. Burton Terry, that they was looking to make a whole new league with Burton as the commissioner. Crossville was getting up a team, for sure, and they was already talking to six or seven other towns in Tennessee and a coupla in some nearby states. Burton didn't have to tell me that this was a opper-tunity of your lifetime to get in on the ground floor. But he did anyway.

Bout a month later we had a meeting in Crossville. I must say I was impressed with Burton from the get-go. He was a tall fella, bout six foot two, and though he was wearing glasses by that time, he had played a lil' pro ball at third base when he was younger a course, and more important he had been a GM in pro ball, with the Lookouts down in Chattanooga. He went into selling that crap you spread on a wet ball diamond so you can keep on playing and was suck-cessful at it, but he had the itch to get back into the game in a official capacity again, so there he was starting up a whole league. As for me, right away I liked the feel of it, being a bone-na fide owner of a pro baseball team with voting rights and ever thang. No man was ever happier to write out a check for a hunert grand than me, the cash it took for me to buy the Cookeville franchise.

We had some more meetings and when the dust settled, we had a new league with four teams in Tennessee (Cookeville, Crossville, Tullahoma, and Fayetteville) and one in Florence, Alabama and one in Dalton, Georgia. We named the league the Tennessee-Alabama-Georgia League of Professional Baseball Clubs ... the T-A-G League for short. We dint put "independent" in the name 'cause that weren't important. Pro is pro and ever body who played or worked for the clubs was going to get a pay check jest like they do in the major leagues. It was already the end of March when we got ever thang sorted out and all the teams got their ante-up one hunert grand into the league office which Burton set up on Main Street in Crossville, so we was kinda getting a late start on the season. 'Cause of the dee-la-tory situation it was decided that we would play a 60-game schedule that would run June through September, 12 games 'gainst each team, six home and six on the road. The top four teams would make the playoffs and then fight to the death in two rounds of three-game series to dee-ter-mine the league cham-peen.

That left a few things to get done like finding a place to play, hiring a office staff and a GM and a manager in the dugout, picking a team name, ordering some uniforms and equipment, and finding some players ... plus some other odds and ends stuff like getting a logo, finding a grounds crew and a radio announcer, and deciding what kind of beer and sodi pop we were gonna sell at the ballgame. Two months seemed like plenty of time which jest shows you how lil' I really knew bout being a owner of a pro baseball team.

Looking back on it now I can see it was a miracle we was ready for June 1st but somehow we was. For the most part. The best thang I done to get ready was hire my old junior college coach, Linwood "Pete" Peterson, to be the manager. Pete dint have nut-in much to do in the summer after the spring semester was over nohow, and I was happy to pay him the max salary set by the league, $35,000, which was bout double what he made at Walters State. He brung four of his graduating sophomores with him who done had enough of college by then and signed up five players that jest graduated from his coaching buddy's team over at Lincoln Memorial University in Harrogate up near the Kain-tucky border so that we had our nuclus right there and were able to fill out the roster with some local hot shots and boys we signed at the league tryout camp held in Crossville.

The GM I hired me was a young fella out of some fancy college in the Northeast. He knew all about computers and bidness and pro baseball rules and reg-a-la-shuns and come recommended by all sorts of people already working for pro teams. He said picking the team name was one of the most important things we had to do and we oughta let the public help us so we run a lil' name-the-team contest in the *Commerce*. You wouldna believed the suggestions we got. Cardinals and Rebels and Confederates and even football names like Vols and Cowboys was decent enough but who the hell would want a pro baseball team with a name like the Cookeville Cousins, the Cookeville Crows, the Criminals, the Candy-eaters, or Farm Boys? I was complaining one night about the way the contest was going over at Sis's place, looking through the latest batch of stinkers like Chefs, Cabinet-makers, Tarantulas, and Cuckoo Clocks when Mr. Jessie Blackstone, CEO of Fred's which had just opened they first place in Knoxville, got a mis-chi-vi-ous grin on his face and says, "Fargo, how bout the Cookeville Bar-B-Qers?" I laughed and started to shout "No way, Jose," but then stopped dead in my tracks. You know how your brain can run a million miles a minute when something gets it all fired up? That's what happened then, and I said, "Hush my mouth! You know, that ain't half bad," as I was thinking what could be more wholesome than bar-b-q and that there ain't nut-in ever body in the South loves more than a good pulled pork sammich.

I thought we had that par-tic-lar nut cracked but the GM dint seem to care for it much. He says, "I think you oughta run it past Peterson first and see what he says." So I did and Pete surprised me like a moccasin slithering over your boots in the high grass. "Ain't no way, Fargo," says he. "The kids don't care that much one way or the other but I know they ain't going for the Cookeville Bar-B-Qers. What lunatic proposed that name, anyway?"

"Never mind who come up with the name," says I. "We give the people they shot and it's time for us to pee or get off the pot."

"Well, I'm jest telling you: you name your team, a team in pro ball, the Bar-B-Quers and we'll all be a laughing stock. I don't care if we're in Indy ball or not. A name like that would be a joke. On us. I'm jest telling you."

Pete was so convincing that, well, what he said pulled me up like a sprain in the hammy you might get running after kids who hit your car with dirt clods, and I decided then and there to ditch Bar-B-Qers even though I acted like I was still determined on it. When you are a owner of a pro baseball team sometimes you have to put on a act to let your sub-servants know who's the boss. Like Mr. Steinberger always done. The next day I called a meeting of all the boys before practice. When they was all seated in the bleachers at the Cookeville High field where we was gonna play our home games til we built our new ballpark, I tole them they was gonna have the honor of picking the team's name. I tole them they could pick from the Cardinals, the Rebels, or the Crushers. The last name was my brain shower though I really dint care which name they was gonna pick. I figgered they was all good. A coupla of the boys jumped up and started agitating for one name or the other, so I strolled off down the first base line acting like I needed to check to make sure the bag was 'sactly where it was supposed to be, 90 feet away from home plate, jest to give them some private space in case they was finding my presence too intimidating. A few minutes later Pete waved me over and said they done reached a decision. They tole me what it was, let out a big cheer, and then run out on the field like they was ready for blood. They was all shouting, "Crushers! Let's go Cookeville Crushers! Yeah, we're the bad ass Crushers of Cookeville! Don't mess with the Crushers!" Well, I thought, that's a home run for the owner. It weren't til I seen and heard they reactions to our logo, a batter "crushin' " the ball with a big sweepin' swing, that I realized they'd been a big misunderstanding. ... They thought we done named the team after pro wrasslers and was damned disappointed we dint. What in tarnation, I thought. I got me a team full of boys who love pro wrasslin' more than pro baseball!

For bout half the day it felt like some big fat-assed sonna-va-bitch in shiny underwear had me in a headlock ready to bounce me off the ropes right into a clothesline, but that dint last long. They was too many other things to worry bout. Like the new ballpark we was building out on 42, bout half a mile out of town on some already cleared land I bought from a soybean farmer for bout half a million. I wasn't trying to build us no Taj-my-haul but ever time I had a meetin' with the arky-tec and the genral contractor seems like the cost went up another half mil. And the completion date got moved back a week or so. We started off shooting for the end of August but I quickly realized that was pushing it, even with me promising them a big bonus to get the thing built on time. I dint tell no one but I thought I'll be happy if we get to play in our new ballpark at all this season.

The uniforms was another problem. Dirty Harry Woodward over at Big Oak Sportin' Goods keep promising me the uniforms would be here tomorrow, right up til the night before opening day. They was coming from Rawlings in St. Louis. I finally figgered out Harry was a weak little sissy liar. I got so mad he stayed in the store, with me cussing under my breath, three or four hours after closing time to make us a batch of Crushers tee shirts to wear the next day. By the time the real uniforms got to Cookeville, compliments of UPS, in the middle of July those blue tee shirts was purty shabby, I'll tell ya.

Well, opening day come too fast, to be honest, but at least we was at home and we was readier than the Tullahoma Tractors. They dint even have tee shirts that was all the same. They players wore stuff from whatever they last team was: high school, 'merican Legion, college, men's summer league, who knows whatnot. They was awfully young too. I bet they girl friends shaved more than they did. I mean they legs a course. Bout 55 people showed up to watch the game at $3 a head, and we put on a good show, winning the first game in Crushers history

6-0, behind this skinny left-hanner from Lincoln Memorial named Gary Smith. His fastball couldna bruise yer momma's arm but he could nip the eye lashes off a gnat with his curve and those Tullahoma boys dint touch him all day. We won again the next day 4-2 and pulled out the brooms for the sweep 9-7 the day after that to put us in first place in the T-A-G League by our lonesomes.

The rest of that first year flew by like a car of revenuers hi-tailin' it after moonshiners. We figgered we was cock of the walk after beatin' up on Tullahoma but turns out we was middle of the pack. The Dalton Carper Sweepers—ever body jest called them the Sweepers—had the best pitchin' in the league and the Crossville Black Sox had some of ever thang and was a jest plain mean ball club. Furthersmore, Tullahoma dint stay bad. By August they had some purty orange jerseys, jest like the Tennessee Vols over in Knoxville, and a whole new team to boot. Signed a bunch a players dropped by 'filiated teams. The Florence Rockets and the Fayetteville Stampede brung up the rear and dint make the playoffs. We lost two games to one in the playoffs to Crossville, Dalton beat Tullahoma two to nut-in, and then Dalton beat Crossville two to one for the cham-peen-ship.

Turned out Cookeville wasn't near crazy bout pro baseball as me. We averaged bout 75 fans per game but they was some good reasons for that. The new ballpark dint get finished til half way through October. Which meant we stayed put at the high school all season. The beer choice dint take long 'cause the school board dispermitted the sale of beer all together. The bad thang was we found out from the other teams in the T-A-G League that the beer drinkers like pro baseball a lot more than the sodi pop drinkers. We also dint have enough time to sell much advertising for the yearbook or scorecards or our games on the radio, though we did find some sponsors to pay for wooden signs we got to hang on the outfield fences. Mostly lawyers, insurance, banks, and a course Fred's Bar-B-Q, which was going gang busters all over the state by then. Never the less, overall the season was a suck-sess, 'cording to my GM. "Most new Indy leagues don't make it through the first season, certainly not with all their teams intact. We did." The proof we done good, he said, was that our playoffs was wrote down in *Baseball 'merica*. That shows they was starting to take us serious.

At the end of the year when we had to figger up all the money that gone out and come back in, things was a lil' uneven. Miller Field come in around six and a half million and the entrance roads and parking lot was another coupla hunert grand. We spent bout a quarter mil on salaries, $16,000 to rent the high school field, $20,000 on uniforms and equipment, and bout 45 grand on rental vans, motel rooms, and meals for the games on the road. Countin' the money for the league entry fee but not the money for Miller Field which the accountant said we had to dee-pre-shate over time, we figgered the loss was somewhat upwards of half a million for the first year.

We 'spected things to be more lewk-ra-tive in year two but they really wasn't. Seems like the carpet mills in town bought the Sweepers they own bus to ride around in, them being dee-fendin' league champs and all, and so I thought ain't no way I'm gonna let Dalton, Georgia, act no better than Cookeville, Tennessee, so we got us a bus too and had our logo and "Cookeville Crushers Pro Ball, T-A-G League" painted on both sides of it. That took our travelin' 'spenses up a notch, and so did the league's decision to add a third umpire for ever game. Turned out we wasn't done with the new ballpark neither. Somehow, somebody forgot to include a locker room for the visiting team. Crossville was the first team to come to Cookeville that year, and they acted like we done forgot they locker room on purpose, jest to insult them. I wisht to hell we had now. They made a big fuss about it to Burton Terry, and all of a sudden he was Bowie Coon hisself, fined us a hunert grand, gave our locker room to the other T-A-G League teams, and made our players use a trailer in the parking lot til we got the other locker room built.

Since Crossville and us is so close, geographic-wise, they was bound to be our worst rivals. Them being such bastards jest sealed the cake. We had us a real baseball brawl with them in August with beanballs and pileups and fans throwing stuff out the stands and player rejections by the umpires. I wouldna be lying if I tole you that after that ever Crusher player and fan hated ever Black Sox player and fan.

We made the playoffs again and lost again in the first round and dang if Dalton dint win the whole thang again. At least Crossville dint win it. The T-A-G League was in *Baseball 'merica* that whole season, but it dint seem quite as cool as before when a lot of the news was bout Florence runnin' out of money and not payin' they bills. They had a bad team, a worst high school field, and no fans, and they give up the ghost with two weeks to go. The next summer McMinnville took they place and was known as the McGillas. For some reason they mascot was a gorilla, even though ever body knows they ain't no gorillas in Tennessee, 'cept maybe in the Knoxville Zoo. After Florence dropped out, they was no team from Alabama in the league no more, but we figgered it was best to stick with the same name so as not to confuse the fans.

As for us, the Cookeville Crushers, we seemed to get stuck in reverse. McMinnville beat us out for the last spot in the playoffs in the third year, and even though we moved up to third place behind Crossville and Dalton in year four, we jest could not seem to get over the camel's hump. We was still bleeding money too. Although we dint draw at Miller Field like Dalton or Crossville did at they places, the fans that did come out drunk a fair amount of Pabst Blue Ribbon and they ate enough Fred's Bar-B-Q ever game to feed Napoleon's army. Still, something had to be done to turn the ship around or we was never gonna draw enough to make the Crushers pay off, so much as it hurt me to pull a Steinberger on my old college coach I let Pete Peterson go as our manager 'cause they's a old saying in pro baseball: "You cain't fire the owner."

By this time I done made some friends with the 'lanta Braves who ever now and a blue moon would send they scouts sniffing around our games. They liked our new ballpark and the bar-b-q which we never charged 'em for, and they even signed one of our boys to go help them fill out one of they Single A rosters one year. To stay on my good side they sent us one of they players who washed out in Triple A to take over for Pete as my manager. That spring he brung in a bundle of players with 'filiated experience, and all of a sudden I had me a Indy League powerhouse. We started out hot and stayed hot. By the end of August they was no way no team was gonna catch us unless the blue-bonnet plague sweep through our dugout like news that a sexy blond in the stands was asting where the players went after the games to have a beer or somethin' stronger … or naw-ti-er. The dang tragedy of it all was that the people in Cookeville still wasn't coming to enough of our games, unless the hated Crossville Black Sox was in town, and we couldna jest play them all the time. We walked all over Tullahoma in round one of the playoffs, and then after Crossville beat McMinville, we stomped Crossville too in the finals to win our first T-A-G cham-peen-ship. It was double the pleasure and double the fun that by winning we made Crossville be the losers. It don't get no better than that.

After all the celebrating I had a sit down with the 'countant who tole me what I was afraid of: we still had more money go out for the summer than come in and I was in danger of becoming ... well, jest a lil' bit rich. Another coupla cham-peen-ship seasons like this one and I'd be plumb broke. That made my head do some spinning, I'll tell ya, and caused me to do some real soul surfing.

I worried myself sick for bout another month and finally slunk off to my sister's house which by this time was a cotton pickin' mansion woulda made Elvis proud to live in. Jessie was there too and we talked a coupla hours with me laying all my cards on the table. I wasn't looking for no loan or charity but thought they might want to invest in my pro baseball team. After Sis and Jessie looked at each other for bout five minutes like they knew what they was both thinking without speaking a solitary word, Jessie says to me, "Fargo, we ... ahem ... don't have no interest in investing in the Crushers or no other pro ball team. But ... we would like to invite you to buy a Fred's franchise ... at a family discount a course."

I bout cried when I admitted to myself the situation, and although I said I would think bout they offer, I knew right away I was gonna take them up on it. The next day I bought a Fred's franchise with half of the money I had left and tole my GM to put the Crushers up for sale on the QT.

When you win a cham-peen-ship in pro baseball, ever body gets a big fancy ring at the first game the next spring. What I did was put in a rush order on the rings, and we give 'em out at a big party at Miller Field during the major league World Series. It was probably gonna be my last purchase as owner of the Crushers so I dint scrimp on the quality of the rings.

My sister and brother-in-law was kind enough to give me the first Fred's franchise in 'lanta with rights to the territory, and one day in January I was on a plane flying down there from Knoxville where we done had us a meeting. I was minding my own bidness, reading a rest-a-ront magazine, when the fella acrosst the aisle ast me bout the big ring on my left hand. After I tole him how I come by it, he says, "Gee, I'm always jealous as hell when I see a pro baseball team cham-peen-ship ring on another fella's finger. That sure is a purty one. How much did it cost?"

"This ring here? How much did it cost?" says I.

"This ring cost me a whole lot of Bar-B-Q!"

# An Unhappy Death

Dennis Moeller was sitting up straight, alertly steering his green '78 Nova over the tortuous and slippery roads of the Virginia countryside. A light snow had started to fall, frosting the road like a layer of icing on a cake. The sky was darkening quickly, further reducing visibility. Compounding the difficulty of driving in such conditions was the fact that Dennis was almost completely unfamiliar with the territory he was traversing. He had been over these roads once before several years earlier, but the trip had been made at night, and so he had practically no road marks or signposts in his memory to guide him. Thus, he drove warily, considerably slower than his passenger would have.

When the road forked or intersected, he had to ask directions of his passenger, his girlfriend Julie, slumped against her door in the front seat. Julie would murmur a perfunctory "Straight," "Left," or "Right," hardly turning her dark-haired head away from the foggy window in her door to do so, and then would resume her brooding that had engulfed the car in an unnatural quiet since she had awakened from a fitful nap outside Winston-Salem an hour before. After a few unsuccessful attempts to engage her in conversation, Dennis had decided to let her brown study run its course. Although he couldn't of course read her mind, he was pretty certain that Julie was thinking about the rapidly failing health of her father, Josh Hector, the former big league baseball star, whom they were traveling to visit on the advice of Josh's doctor. If she wanted privacy, he thought, the least he could do would be to respect her wish. She had, after all, asked him to come with her–though it meant using up his vacation– and that in itself indicated both how much his mere presence comforted her and how much she thought she had a right to ask him.

Diverting his eyes from the dark landscape into which he was driving, Dennis stole a glance at the athletically-built woman across from him dressed in a gray sweat shirt and white corduroy jeans. Her pretty face and big brown eyes were turned away from him, but her sitting position accentuated her body and caused a rush of desire in him. Dennis thought back to the day he had first met Julie.

As head of one of the branch public libraries in Asheville, North Carolina, Dennis had had to replace five years ago one of the part-timers on his staff. Julie Hector was the young woman he had wound up hiring. Just by chance Julie had been in the library that hot summer day, looking through the "help wanteds" of the various nearby city and community newspapers that the library carried. After graduating from UNC-Asheville and teaching elementary school for a frustrating year, Julie had discovered that she loathed teaching, and she retired from the profession. From that time until she had been hired by Dennis, she had worked at a succession of low-paying dead-end jobs, barely keeping body and soul together. Noticing the procession of applicants passing back and forth through the door of Dennis' office that day, Julie had deduced what was happening and decided to go immediately after the position—whatever it was—before somebody else got hired. Turning her unpreparedness into an asset, she had assaulted Dennis with an apoplexy of apology and embarrassment at her seeking an employment interview in such an unprofessional manner. On his part, Dennis had immediately admired not only her assertiveness but her prettiness and her figure as well— her red shorts displaying a pair of long shapely legs—and had promised not to hire anybody until he talked to her the next day. As Julie had backed out of his office, thanking him profusely, Dennis had chuckled and decided then and there that unless her qualifications were egregiously insufficient, he would hire her for the part-time position. Shortly thereafter, Julie was not only working in the library science profession, but she was dating the area's brightest young library administrator, one who had his eye on nothing less than the directorship of the entire Asheville public library system—a position which promised to be vacant soon since the current director was nearing retirement.

Dennis' attention was snapped back to the present as Julie suddenly slid across the front seat and snuggled up next to him. She put her arm around his shoulders and smiled half-heartedly into his face as she asked, "Well, what are you in such a black mood about?"

"Me...? In a black mood...? Look who's talking!" he said with mock astonishment. He immediately regretted reminding her of her burden. Her face lost its glimmer. She took her arm from around him.

"Julie, what's the matter?" he asked softly.

"Oh, Denny," she said, covering her face with her hands, "I'm scared."

For a few moments they rode in silence again, the swish of the windshield wipers and the hum of the car's motor the only sounds audible.

In her distress Julie drew her body together somewhat into a ball and began rocking slightly, as a sick or frightened child might. She seemed a bit pathetic to Dennis, and he was touched and more than a little curious. He had a strong desire to hear her express her innermost feelings, and he wanted then to draw her into intimate conversation.

"Julie, your father has been ill for some time now. You've known that. Thank goodness he hasn't been in a lot of pain. I know it's hard to imagine living without both of your parents, but you won't be alone. You'll always have me.... That is, as long as you want me."

She looked at him with sheer amazement. "I'm not afraid of my father dying, of living without him.... I'm afraid of his dying unhappy."

"Unhappy...? Why, what's your father got to be unhappy about? He's lived a full and productive life. A college football hero, a major league baseball star, a big hero in the World Series, made a lot of money in the stock market. ... From what you've told me he's practically a rich man—even if his daughter is too proud and independent to take one red cent."

"You don't understand, Denny."

From the scowl on her face Dennis finally began to realize how seriously she was taking the idea of her father dying an unhappy man. He remembered the first time he had visited, a couple of years earlier.

The visit had come about because he and Julie had begun to think about marriage, and she had decided it was time for her father and Dennis to meet. Julie had tried to prepare Dennis, hinting quizzically about Josh being argumentative and difficult, and it all having something to do with his baseball career, but she changed the subject when Dennis pressed her for a further explanation. Dennis had assumed she had been referring to nothing much more than the normal moodiness that many older people experience when life seems to pass them by and their once healthy bodies begin to fail them. Josh Hector might especially feel that way, Dennis had figured, since he had been so athletic as a younger man.

Still, Dennis had been ill at ease from the start. Mr. Hector had been barely polite and had generally ignored him during their first visit. He and Julie had discussed local people and things, leaving Dennis completely out of the conversations and feeling as awkward as a pimply-faced boy on his first date. It wasn't until—in desperation—Dennis had mentioned Josh's playing days with the old St. Louis Cards that the old man had paid him any attention at all. And then it had been only to ask sneeringly what the hell Dennis knew about all that. Taken aback by the old man's hostility but encouraged nevertheless, Dennis had repeated in flattering terms what he had heard Julie say about Josh's career: the lifetime batting average over .300, over 400 stolen bases, one of the highest career fielding percentages ever for an outfielder, his outstanding play in three World Series. The old man didn't make much of a reply, but from then on Dennis had felt a grudging acceptance from him. Going over the entire visit Dennis could not find anything in what he had observed to be Josh Hector's life that would cause the old ballplayer great distress, unless it was the fact that today's players made so much more money than he did as a young Cardinal. Dennis recalled now how angry Josh had become when he had mentioned jokingly near the end of their visit while Julie had been out shopping that even today's mediocre benchwarmer was probably on his way to becoming a millionaire. Josh had gone into a rage about the modern ballplayers and all the fuss made over them, cursing the "overrated and gutless amateurs who couldn't have carried my jockstrap." But it made no sense for Josh Hector, financially quite "well off," to envy the money of anybody else, and Dennis haltingly attempted to continue the conversation to get at what Julie was worried about.

"Josh isn't concerned about money, is he, Julie? I mean, having enough to leave you so you'll be taken of...? As if you can't take care of yourself."

"Don't be absurd. My father's practically rich."

"Yes, I know. But I guess you worry about things like that when you think about not being around anymore. Well, if it's not you, what is it then? Is it his pride?"

She looked at him searchingly then. "Yes. It is a matter of pride," she said finally.

To conceal his pleasure at perceiving the motive behind the old man's behavior, Dennis used an exaggerated tone of exasperation to exclaim, "Well, that's silly, for your father to care one whit how much Reggie Jackson or some other big shot in knickers makes. Everybody knows those guys are overpaid for what they do, that they aren't worth the kind of money they make. Nobody is worth that kind of money just for playing a game. So your father has nothing to be ashamed of for making peanuts compared to..."

"Ashamed! What are you talking about, Dennis? My father despises money, just like I do," she hissed at him. "What a moronic thing to say! My father was a great baseball player..."

"Yeah, I know he was. I understand that."

"No. ... No, you don't understand. You have no idea how good my father was. Do you really know the details of Josh Hector's career? Have you ever looked up his record in *The Baseball Encyclopedia*? Compared it to other players who are supposed to be as good as him? Would you even understand what it means to bat over .300 for nine different seasons? No, you don't understand how great a ballplayer my father was. You're just like everybody else. He's an old man now, in fact, he's dying, so it doesn't matter anymore. Pretty soon he'll be just another forgotten old-timer. And it isn't fair! They've screwed him for one little thing, and they're not ever going to let him into the Hall of Fame, and he's going to die so miserable because of it." Julie had begun to cry, and when she had finished speaking in a torrent of bitterness she continued to sob, her face covered again by her hands.

Dennis was shaken by her outburst, and a wave of confused feelings—surprise, anger, embarrassment, jealously—swept over him. Through them all a perversely delightful resentment began to surface, and he indulged it for a moment by imagining that Julie was a perfect stranger of no concern to him, and that he would in the next moment lash back at her, her sobbing, and her father's enormous vanity. But he fought back the sensation. He began to apologize and to explain, but she held up her hand and slowly shook her head.

By this time they were only a few miles from the home of Josh Hector, and Julie composed herself enough to give the final directions. When they finally arrived, they found the stately old colonial house completely dark. Neither was in a hurry to leave the car, and so they sat there staring at the tall white columns of the front of the house.

Dennis wanted to talk to Julie, but he hardly knew what to say anymore and was afraid of upsetting her again. Julie seemed to be lost in her thoughts. He broke the silence.

"I never realized how much this Hall of Fame business meant to you and your father."

He waited for her to say something, but she only stared blankly towards the dark house looming over them. When he was about to lose patience and speak again, she finally began to speak.

"As a matter of justice my father should be a member of the Hall of Fame. He has the credentials, better ones than dozens of men who have been elected over him.

"After he retired, he was confident that he would be elected, but they passed him over every time because he had the balls to tell sportswriters to go to hell. After a certain length of time they even quit putting his name on the ballot. That hurt my father deeply; nobody will ever know how much grief he suffered because of that. When you know you deserve something, when you've put your whole life and heart and soul into something and you've earned it and people still don't recognize what you've done, then you have a right to be angry and bitter. My father never wanted any special consideration. He just wanted to be treated fairly, and the fair thing would have been to give my father a place of honor alongside the other great baseball players in history. When they took his name off the ballot, my father became a changed man. He started having problems getting along with my mom, he lost interest in just about everything, and he just didn't want to do anything anymore. Then a few years before I met you, they made up this Veterans Committee to put in people who had been overlooked. My father got his hopes up all over again. He was certain that they'd admit their mistake and take him right away. But they only seem interested in blacks and umpires, and the few old white players they've been picking can't hold a candle to my father. It's been the same old story again, except that this time my father is an old man with a broken heart. And every year the Veterans Committee has passed him up, they're ripped out another little piece of his heart. … And now … it looks like he's not going to ever make it. I can't stand it that he's going to die having been cheated of the most important thing in the world to him."

"Isn't there some other governing body we could appeal to to get your father a thorough review? I mean, if this Veterans Committee is obviously falling short—"

"No, Denny. The Veterans Committee is it. There's some baseball history organization that sent him a letter saying they were lobbying to get him selected, buy they probably don't have any influence. Besides, I'm afraid it's too late now. The Veterans Committee doesn't vote until spring of each year, and Dr. Fleming said Dad is probably not going to recover."

They sat together in the darkness for a while longer but soon began to feel the cold. Then they went up to the house.


It had snowed off and on for three days since their arrival, and Dennis and Julie had stayed almost the whole time inside the house, practically in a single room. They had found Josh and his nurse living in the study. He rested on a couch, and she slept on a cot. The rest of the 13 rooms were empty and closed off. The nurse explained with a shrug that months earlier, before he had been stricken, the old man had sold and given away the contents of the rest of the house.

The old man lay on the French Provincial couch, drifting into and out of a semiconscious and restive state, with his daughter constantly at his side. As Dennis watched him hour after hour their first day, it occurred to him that Josh's house-emptying had been an appropriately symbolic act but a damned inconsiderate one too. When he had left the house that afternoon, despite Julie's glare of disapproval, to drive to town for two additional cots, he had felt tremendously relieved to be away from the gloomy house full of mourning and impending death.

By the morning of the third day Dennis was finding the vigil that Julie expected him to keep with her at Josh's bedside to be almost unbearable. Her refusal to be drawn into conversation about any topic except the unchanging condition of her father frustrated and bored him, though he also admired her strength and devotion at the same time. The nurse, Mrs. Vargas, a competent but dull functionary, had told them that Dr. Fleming would be stopping by that morning to check on Josh. Longing for some congeniality and companionship, Dennis had decided to engage the doctor in some conversation on his way up to the house. Although there was still enough firewood in the house to heat the study for two or three more days, the idea of physical exertion appealed to Dennis, and he went out to the carriage and tool shed to chop wood.

He had been working steadily for 15 minutes, enjoying the invigorating warmth his body produced under his heavy coat, when Dr. Fleming started his light blue Caprice up the driveway. Dennis laid the axe down and waved the car to a stop. Dr. Fleming, himself only a few years younger than Josh, was in robust health. His green eyes sparkled as he rolled down his window and greeted Dennis with a pleasant smile.

"Dr. Fleming?" Dennis asked.

"Yes, sir. Precisely. And you must be Julie's friend."

"Right. Denny Moeller," he said, extending his hand.

"I'm pleased to meet you, Denny," the doctor said. "But what are doing out here in the cold?"

"Oh … I was chopping some firewood over there by the tool shed, but I really … uh … just kind of wanted to talk to you for a few minutes … before you go up to the house."

"I see. Well, why don't you get into the car, and we can have a little private chat right here."

Dr. Fleming shut off the motor and reached over to unlock the door on the passenger's side. Dennis climbed in and noticed in the middle of the seat Dr. Fleming's bulky black bag, which looked exactly like the kind he thought still existed only in old movies.

"Is everything okay up at the house?" asked the doctor.

"Oh, yeah, sure. I mean, Josh is about the same around the clock. He sleeps most of the time, and when he wakes up he's not very alert or coherent. Julie has practically taken over for Mrs. Vargas. She talks to him and tries to feed him, but I don't think he is very conscious of it."

The doctor studied Dennis' face and then asked, "How's Julie taking it?"

"Pretty well."

"I'm a little concerned about her. I tried not to alarm her when I called about Josh, but I didn't want to raise any false hopes either."

"Don't worry about her, Doctor. Julie got the message. She knows her dad is dying."

The doctor frowned and began to toy with the handle of his black bag. "Julie grieved deeply when her mother died, and so did Josh. Margaret's death drew them closer together; having each other helped pull them both through, made them realize how important they are to each other."

"I thought Julie and her dad were always tight."

"Well, they were. It's just that Josh had really wanted a boy, and he was never able to hide his disappointment very well. Julie never told you that?"

"No, not really."

"The funny thing is he couldn't have produced a more athletic child. Julie was some basketball player."

"Really?"

"Yes, indeed. She averaged over twenty-five points a game for the high school, and she won a scholarship to play at Asheville. Made All-American there two years. Didn't she ever tell you about that?"

"Well, yeah. I knew she played, but she never told me that she excelled like that."

"Oh, yes sir. She took right after her dad in athletics. Tough, aggressive, smart. I think she has the strength to come through this okay, but we need to watch her closely. She's by herself, you know; no brothers or sisters, no close relatives to speak of. Josh took care of that."

"What about Mr. Hector, Doctor? I only met him once, a couple of years ago. I know how highly Julie thinks of him, and I'm sorry that I didn't get to know him better."

At this the doctor frowned again and sighed ponderously as if Dennis's remarks had brought to mind regrettable memories. "If you only met Josh Hector for the first time a few years ago," he said, "there is no way for you to have known the real man. By the time you met him, he had become a totally different man and less of the wonderful person he had always been. Josh suffered—to his mind—a terrible disappointment that tragically came to be repeated year after year. He felt cheated by petty politics—some grudge about something he said long ago—out of an important honor, election to the Hall of Fame, and the injustice he felt made him bitter and angry. He lost sight of all the good things in his life, complained all the time, and railed against those he felt were responsible. He drove his friends away and even lost Julie for a time. It's gnawed away at him over the years until he's finally … well … he's become a defeated old man."

"Doctor, are you trying to tell me that Josh Hector is suffering from a broken heart?"

"Well, young man, after a few years in this business you learn that the body is a marvelous thing that can take a tremendous amount of wear and tear, but that doesn't matter if hope dies, if the human spirit surrenders."

There was a charged pause and then, as if anticipating Dennis' thoughts, Dr. Fleming continued, speaking directly to them.

"Josh is medically ill. He's had a stroke, but there is little we could do for him at a hospital that we can't do here. Warmth, cleanliness, and the medication are the main things, and Mrs. Vargas is able to attend to all that. I see no reason to go against Josh's wishes and move him to the county hospital. On the other hand, if Josh hadn't given up ... who's to say?"

"It certainly looks like he just decided to quit. I mean, selling everything in the house like that. That's spooky."

"Actually, he sold very little. Gave most of it away. He started out just giving away the souvenirs, trophies, and paraphernalia he had saved from his baseball days, but then he kept going and gave away all the rest."

"Boy, you'd never know by walking through that empty house that the owner was a rich man."

"He's not ... not anymore. He also cashed in his stocks and bonds, gave the money to charity."

Dennis was stunned by this news, and his eyes were drawn towards the big colonial house and the single chimney from which gray smoke streamed.

"Such generosity is more like the old Josh. It's a pity you never knew him."

Dennis thanked the doctor for his time and got out to finish his exercise. He walked over to the woodpile deep in thought and was already mechanically chopping wood when the doctor walked into Josh Hector's house.

The following afternoon a phone call interrupted Dennis who was reading a book of stories by Ring Lardner in what was left of Josh's study. He was sitting on an old cushionless maple chair by the window in the former dining room where the light was good. It surprised him when Mrs. Vargas came into the room to say that the call was for him. To reach the phone located at the end of the hall on the first floor, Dennis had to pass through the study, where the old ballplayer lingered halfway between life and death. Dennis could see that Julie had been dozing in the armchair pulled up next to her father's bed, and they exchanged questioning glances without speaking as he walked by. They had spoken very little in the past two days, but Julie knew that the call must be about something important and that Dennis and she would have to discuss it. She heard Dennis talking softly and indistinctly in the hall for just a few minutes before he hung up and returned to the study.

She sat up stiffly and waited for him to begin. She seemed to notice a gleam of excitement in his eyes and a certain impatience.

"That was Laura. She said Mr. Delancey is dead. He had a heart attack the day after we left."

"Oh no! ... But that means..."

"Yes, they've already starting interviewing for a replacement."

She wanted to go up to him and put her arms around him and have him hold her tight and tell her everything was okay and he'd never ever leave her, but the physical and emotional drain of the past few days had exhausted her and she suddenly felt very old and very tired and incapable of the slightest exertion. Dennis watched as her face flickered momentarily to life and then returned to the stoic, impassive expression he had seen so much of lately. Her eyes glazed over as she seemed to stare across the room at nothing in particular.

"Laura said I have until Friday noon to get back for an interview. This is the opportunity we've been waiting for, Julie. You know I hate to leave you at a time like this, but they won't wait past Friday. There has to be somebody in control there, especially with the big budgetary and funding meetings coming up. You understand that, don't you?"

She didn't respond in any way, so after a moment or two he left the room. He quickly gathered his things, discussed a few practical matters of importance with Mrs. Vargas—leaving his Visa card with her for Julie—and left the house without saying goodbye. As he drove away, a light snow began to fall again, and he told himself before he had reached the dirt road that ran past the Hector driveway that he had nothing to feel guilty about.

The interview for the directorship of the Asheville Public Library went well, but Dennis did not get the job. He handled the disappointment well, and Monday afternoon after lunch his staff at the branch threw him a surprise consolation party.

Dennis had tried to call Julie several times since his return to Asheville but had been unable to get through. Monday evening, still unable to reach the Hector residence, he began to try to contact Dr. Fleming. Around nine o'clock he finally caught the doctor at home. Dr. Fleming told him that the old ballplayer had finally passed away Friday morning and had been buried the next day, there being no mourners to speak of to hold a period of visitation for.

When Dennis asked about Julie, Dr. Fleming said that she was still going through a difficult period of the grieving process, but for him not to worry too much as he was looking after her and seeing to it that she received what she needed most: rest and some time to herself to recover from her sorrow. Dennis thanked the doctor for his concern and trouble and told him to assure Julie that there was no need for her to worry about coming back to work until she was ready, that everyone would be happy to cover for her.

Determined that he would not be passed over again for the director's job, over the next several days Dennis plunged back into his work with renewed zeal. He started working overtime, a couple of hours past closing hour each night, trying to make his branch stand out. Although as an administrator he rarely had time to read anything not pertaining to his job, one night about a week after talking to Dr. Fleming, Dennis returned from supper to find the latest copy of *The Sporting News* on his desk, opened to the obituary page with a circle drawn with a red pen around the headline, FORMER

STAR "HOST" HECTOR DEAD. He picked up the paper and read the obituary:

*Josh "Host" Hector died at his Simplicity, Virginia, home Friday, December 10. He was 68. Hector enjoyed an outstanding career, hitting over .300 nine times, with a career high of .348. His lifetime average was .309. From 1941 to 1951 he played with the St. Louis Cardinals, helping them to three National League pennants and two World Series Championships.*

*He is best remembered for his aggressiveness and hustle, exemplified by his famous steal of second base and mad dash all the way home on the catcher's throwing error to score the winning run in the sixth game of the '47 Series. He was dubbed "Host" by sportswriters for his remark that sportswriters "are nothing but slimy parasites that make their living sucking blood out of ballplayers."*

He finished his career with the Philadelphia Phillies in 1952 and the Washington Senators in 1953-4 and still holds several Cardinal team records. He is survived by his daughter, Julie Hector, also of Simplicity, Virginia.

There was a photo to accompany the text. It depicted a young Josh Hector sliding across home plate in a cloud of dust. Dennis realized with a jolt that he had seen the picture before somewhere: Josh sitting on top of home, one hand raised in the air, the other palm down in the dust; the umpire poised to signal "safe"; the helpless catcher in front of the plate waiting for the tardy throw. He thought that the photo must be famous for him to have seen it before. As he examined the photo, he felt distracted, then realized that something about the obituary disturbed him.

The notice referred to Simplicity as Julie's place of residence. He tried to tell himself that it was a meaningless instance of reportorial laziness, but he couldn't shake the sinking feeling that it was a premonition. Somehow, for some reason, he began to feel with greater and greater certainty that he would never see her again.

He did see her again, once more, on cable television, about a year and a half after he received her last letter, informing him that she'd begun a relationship with someone new and asking "for both their sakes" not to contact her ever again. After Josh had died, she herself suffered a breakdown, and it was only through Dr. Fleming's kind ministrations that she recovered as quickly as she did. While she had lain exhausted on the couch on which her father had so recently passed away (putting Mrs. Vargas back to work), she had decided to remain in Simplicity and live in the old Hector home. When she had gotten better, she and Dr. Fleming had gone out shopping for furniture with which to furnish the house. Luckily, they had even found some of the things Josh had given away, including much of his baseball memorabilia, and had been able to buy them back. In late January Julie had begun subbing at the county junior high and helping with the girls' basketball team.

Several times Dennis had come close to dropping everything to make an impetuous and uninvited trip to Simplicity to make a personal appeal to her, but his pride and sense of practicality always intervened before he got his roadmap out. His image of Julie began to fade, and he found it increasingly difficult, especially after her last letter and the news of the new boyfriend, to picture her facial features with any clarity.

He was at home one hot Saturday afternoon in August, trying to stay cool and paying hardly any attention at all, when he looked up at his television set and recognized her. He immediately turned up the volume to the sound of enthusiastic applause. Standing on a stage behind a podium topped with microphones and decorated in front with a logo of pillars, laurel leaves, and a baseball, she was accepting a plaque from a very distinguished and well-dressed official. She was dressed in a smart black suit he had never seen on her before, and though she was as pretty as ever the brooding expression in her eyes caused him to shudder. When the applause died down, she moved to the microphones: "You will never know how much this would have meant to my father when he was alive and how little it means now that he is dead." With that said, she moved quickly away from the microphones, out of the television picture, and out of his life forever.